"Tell me that you'll go to the Christmas party with me. It's the event of the season."

"James, do you think—"

"Yes, I do," he said as he leaned close. Scarlett watched him in shock as his lips descended, as he kissed her.

Only then did she close her eyes and give in to the feelings he aroused. She went from surprised to turned on in a nanosecond. Scarlett wasn't sure how long the kiss lasted, only that she wanted it to last forever.

When he pulled back she went with him. Just for a second, but long enough to show that she liked it.

And he knew, darn him. He smiled slowly as he looked into her eyes.

"I take it that was a yes?"

D0727753

Dear Reader,

Welcome back to Brody's Crossing, Texas! Christmas is such a wonderful time of the year. I just can't imagine being stranded in a strange town, far away from family and friends, but that's exactly what happens to Scarlett, the heroine of this story. It doesn't take long for the spunky hairstylist to make friends, though, even when local attorney James Brody advises her that a few lawsuit-happy folks aren't happy with their hair. Soon almost all the residents have warmed up to the Atlanta native, who is on her way to California to become the next "stylist to the stars."

Although Brody's Crossing is a fictional place, I tried to incorporate many of the traditions, decorations and sentiments of the Christmas season in Texas. I hope you enjoy visiting the town during your holidays. I would love to hear from you via my Web site, www.victoriachancellor.com.

Best wishes to you and your family at this joyous, amazing and sometimes hectic time of year. I know I'm looking forward to seeing the look of wonder on my new granddaughter's face as she gazes at the Christmas tree and tears into her many presents! Have a very happy New Year, and I hope 2008 brings you everything you desire.

Warmest holiday greetings,

Victoria Chancellor

Texan for the Holidays
VICTORIA CHANCELLOR

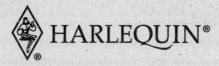

HARLEQUIN®

TORONTO • NEW YORK • LONDON
AMSTERDAM • PARIS • SYDNEY • HAMBURG
STOCKHOLM • ATHENS • TOKYO • MILAN • MADRID
PRAGUE • WARSAW • BUDAPEST • AUCKLAND

If you purchased this book without a cover you should be aware
that this book is stolen property. It was reported as "unsold and
destroyed" to the publisher, and neither the author nor the
publisher has received any payment for this "stripped book."

ISBN-13: 978-0-373-75194-5
ISBN-10:   0-373-75194-X

TEXAN FOR THE HOLIDAYS

Copyright © 2007 by Victoria Chancellor Huffstutler.

All rights reserved. Except for use in any review, the reproduction or
utilization of this work in whole or in part in any form by any electronic,
mechanical or other means, now known or hereafter invented, including
xerography, photocopying and recording, or in any information storage
or retrieval system, is forbidden without the written permission of the
publisher, Harlequin Enterprises Limited, 225 Duncan Mill Road,
Don Mills, Ontario M3B 3K9, Canada.

This is a work of fiction. Names, characters, places and incidents are
either the product of the author's imagination or are used fictitiously,
and any resemblance to actual persons, living or dead, business
establishments, events or locales is entirely coincidental.

This edition published by arrangement with Harlequin Books S.A.

® and TM are trademarks of the publisher. Trademarks indicated with
® are registered in the United States Patent and Trademark Office, the
Canadian Trade Marks Office and in other countries.

www.eHarlequin.com

Printed in U.S.A.

ABOUT THE AUTHOR

Victoria Chancellor married a visiting Texan in her home state of Kentucky thirty-five years ago, and has lived in the Lone Star State for thirty-two years after a brief stay in Colorado. Her household includes her husband, four cats, a very spoiled miniature pinscher, an atrium full of tortoises, turtles and toads, and lots of visiting wild critters. Last year she was blessed with both a new son-in-law and a granddaughter. Her former careers include fine jewelry sales, military security and financial systems analysis. She would love to hear from you via her Web site, www.victoriachancellor.com, or P.O. Box 852125, Richardson, TX 75085-2125.

Books by Victoria Chancellor

HARLEQUIN AMERICAN ROMANCE

844—THE BACHELOR PROJECT
884—THE BEST BLIND DATE IN TEXAS
955—THE PRINCE'S COWBOY DOUBLE
959—THE PRINCE'S TEXAS BRIDE
992—THE C.E.O. & THE COOKIE QUEEN
1035—COMING HOME TO TEXAS
1098—DADDY LESSONS
1172—TEMPORARILY TEXAN*

*Brody's Crossing

Don't miss any of our special offers. Write to us at the following address for information on our newest releases.

Harlequin Reader Service
U.S.: 3010 Walden Ave., P.O. Box 1325, Buffalo, NY 14269
Canadian: P.O. Box 609, Fort Erie, Ont. L2A 5X3

To my sister and brother-in-law,
Peggy and John Garrett, who celebrated
fifty years of marriage in 2007. Happy anniversary!

Acknowledgments

Thanks to my longtime hairstylist, Erin Grassie,
and stylist Charlie Price, for answering my "hair"
questions. Any mistakes are mine.
Thanks to longtime mechanic for my '78 Firebird,
Quint Delconte of Rallye Automotive,
for suggestions of a cracked piston ring.
And thanks to fellow writer and good friend
Rebecca Russell, for visiting Graham, Texas, and the
courthouse with me on a blustery winter day.

Chapter One

Saturday, December 1, 2007

"California, here I come," Scarlett shouted out the window of her aging Benz into the Texas prairie. No one was around to hear, but that was okay. Before long, lots of people would know Scarlett, hairstylist to the stars. She rolled up the window, feeling refreshed from the brisk, cool air.

She was making good time, despite the wrong turn she'd taken back in Dallas. And she'd missed Interstate 35W because she'd been surrounded by huge gravel-hauler trucks. Instead of backtracking, Scarlet had continued on. Eventually, Texas Highway 114 would intersect westbound Interstate 40, somewhere in Oklahoma.

Over an hour after missing the interstate, she passed a city sign that said Loving and noted the town had just a few small buildings. "I'm not loving Texas right now," she said out loud, and laughed at her joke. She turned up the radio and sang along with U2.

Her smile faded when she looked into the rearview mirror to check on an old truck she'd just passed. It was weaving under the weight of about a thousand chicken crates that looked as if they might fall over at any minute.

But the old truck wasn't the only vehicle with a problem. Black smoke billowed in fat inky spirals from her engine— that noisy diesel combustion thing. She knew just enough about cars to add oil, water and of course, fuel, intermittently. Black smoke could not be good. Not good at all…

She checked the gauges and discovered her engine was red-hot. And her oil gauge needle was not where it was supposed to be. When had that happened?

"Darn it," she murmured as she slowed the Benz and looked for a place to pull off. Up ahead, she spotted a wide, rocky patch of dry brown grass and prickly pear cactus. She'd let the car cool off, add some water and oil from the stash she never left home without, and get to the next service station.

She shut off the engine, then opened her door. The cold air coming out of the north nearly took her breath away. Just then the old truck chugged by. It slowed, and Scarlett felt a moment of panic. Was it safe to be alone out here? She hadn't been afraid traveling by herself all the way from Atlanta, and it was broad daylight.

"Need any help?" a raspy voice called to her. A man leaned out the window and Scarlett could see a leathery, stubbled cheek and some missing teeth.

"No, I'm okay." *I hope. Maybe I should pray….*

"If you need a ride, I can take you to Brody's Crossing."

"Thanks, but my car just needs a rest. I'm adding some oil and we'll be on our way soon."

"Could be blown."

What could be blown? She didn't even want to think about *that* statement! "Um…"

"Well, ride's up to you."

"I appreciate the offer, but I'm prepared for this type of situation." Not that this exact scenario had ever happened before.

"Good luck to you, little gal."

Scarlett stifled her surprise. Little gal? "Is there a service station in Brody's Crossing?" So far, she'd only seen modern convenience stores-slash-filling stations.

"McCaskie's. It's on the main street. Can't miss it."

"Well, thanks again."

"Sure 'nuff," he said, before spitting between his missing teeth. "'Course, Claude may not work on these fur-in cars." Then he put his truck in gear and slowly inched away, crates swaying and chickens squawking.

Fur-in? Oh, he meant foreign. How...quaint. She hoped McCaskie's wasn't as predisposed to American-made.

Scarlett let out a sigh. She was all alone with a broken down *fur-in* car. Oh, well. Worse things could happen.

At least she still had all her teeth.

McCASKIE'S SERVICE STATION was closed for the afternoon. And things had definitely gotten worse.

Oh, she still had her teeth. And she hadn't sprouted any facial hair. But her car sat dying beside the road a little more than halfway to Graham, which she'd learned during her ride to town—in a drafty pickup loaded with Christmas trees—was the county seat and the largest town in the area. She huddled out of the wind next to two old-fashioned pumps, wondering what to do now.

Today was Saturday afternoon. Didn't these people need to drive around, buy gas? The sign on the fingerprint-smudged glass door of McCaskie's simply indicated the place was closed for the afternoon, and advised people to "have fun." What the heck?

Brody's Crossing looked as if it had been designed as a movie set for Holiday Hometown, America, complete with tinsel garlands and peppermint canes swaying from

streetlights in the brisk wind. A few temporary traffic bar-
ricades stood on the sidewalk.

She hoisted her backpack-style purse onto her shoulder,
zipped up her hooded sweatshirt and set off for the central
business district, which she figured was maybe two blocks
long. Three at the most. She'd seen small towns similar to this
when her mother had dragged her around Georgia, antiquing.

Scarlett hated antiquing almost as much as she hated
being stranded in a town where service stations closed on
Saturday afternoons and sidewalks were barricaded.

In just a minute or two she arrived at Clarissa's House of
Style, an old-fashioned "beauty shop" in a brick-and-frame
narrow, long building that might have been a house years
ago. A big picture window lined with multicolored lights and
silver tinsel gave the shop a cheery glow on the blustery day.

Since she only felt at home when she was in a salon,
Scarlett couldn't wait to enter. The smells of shampoo,
conditioner, styling products and even perms. The sight of
dramatic hairstyle posters and fashion magazines to stimu-
late creativity. The subtle chatter of clients and stylists, the
intense concentration of manicurists, and even the gentle
splash of water in the big basins. She loved it all.

As Scarlett stepped into the House of Style, everyone
in the place stopped talking to stare. She focused on the
person closest to the door, whose name tag read Clarissa.

"What can I do for you, hon?" The older lady smiled as
she lifted her penciled brows. Clarissa was slightly over-
weight, well-endowed and middle-aged. Her hair was
blond, teased and sprayed into submission. Her most
defining characteristic, though, was the traditional pink
smock worn by many small-town hairdressers.

Scarlett felt as if she'd walked into every proprietor-
owned salon she'd ever seen—and some where she'd

worked—in Georgia. Then her smile faded. She didn't want to revisit her early years. She wanted to go to California, where stylists wouldn't be caught dead in pink smocks.

"Hi, I'm Scarlett. My car broke down about ten miles away, and I got a ride into town. The service station is closed and I'm trying to figure out what's going on."

"Why, today is the Christmas parade, that's what!" Clarissa answered with a chuckle. "It's just about the biggest event this side of the prom or…homecoming. We're fixing hair for all the holiday princesses!"

For the first time, Scarlett really looked at each person in the salon. Sure enough, although there seemed to be only two stylists, all four chairs were filled, with teenage girls. They looked like little clones. Blond or blondish, with updos and tendrils right out of the 1990s.

Yep, she'd stepped into a time warp. "I see." She sighed and hoped she could talk McCaskie, or someone who knew car repairs, into looking at her Benz, despite the apparent importance of the parade. "I'm not from around here."

"Oh, we figured that one out right away!" the other stylist said with a chuckle.

Scarlett gave her an insincere smile instead of a snappy comment, and turned back to Clarissa. "Is there another garage where someone might look at my car?"

"No, hon, I'm sorry, but Claude McCaskie is about the only one around. He's got a tow truck, but he's using it now over at the high school parking lot. He always pulls the holiday princess float, doesn't he, Venetia?"

"You bet. Every year," the other stylist answered.

"Maybe I could go over to the school and see if he could take some time off to tow my car."

"I've never known Claude to miss the Christmas parade. He takes real pride in helping out. He used to be Santa, you see, but lost weight once he was diagnosed with sugar diabetes and started eating that glycemic index food."

No, Scarlett didn't see, but she needed loyal Claude and his tow truck. "Is the high school very far?" Maybe she could walk over and talk to him.

"Just about half a mile south on the farm-to-market road. But really, hon, I don't think he's going to give up his afternoon. He sure enjoys a good parade."

"I understand, but my car is sitting out there beside the road, and I don't have a lot of options."

Clarissa sighed. "Let me get finished with Shawna's hair and I'll make a phone call out to the school. I might get lucky and find someone who could talk to Claude."

"That would be wonderful. Thank you."

"Have a seat," Clarissa said as she finished Shawna's updo. The girl's face was too small and thin to pull off that style. She needed something simple, preferably short, with just enough volume to frame her eyes.

Please, God, do not let her near blue, sparkly eye shadow, Scarlett silently prayed.

"If I can't get my car repaired, is there a motel or hotel where I can get a room?"

"Well, that's the thing about small towns, hon. They don't always have a Holiday Inn. The Sweet Dreams Motel closed about the time the first George Bush became president, and no one's opened another place since then. Mostly, folks stay with relatives or down in Graham."

"Oh." That was bad. "Do you have any suggestions?"

"Let me think while I finish up with Shawna." Clarissa grabbed a can of fine mist spray and applied it liberally to poor Shawna's old-fashioned, too-mature-for-her updo. Shaking her head at her critical thoughts, Scarlett dug in her backpack for her wallet.

As soon as Clarissa put down the spray, Scarlet handed her her Georgia hairdresser's license. "I didn't mention it earlier, but I'm a stylist also. I'm just passing through on my way to California."

"Why, look at that. So you are." Clarissa smiled and handed the paper back to Scarlett. "I don't suppose you're looking for a job, are you, Sa—?"

"Scarlett. I don't go by that other name," she said just above a whisper. "No, I'm only passing through."

"Well, hon, if you wanted to help with some styling this afternoon, I could trade you a place to stay this weekend. Believe me, Claude McCaskie isn't going to get your car fixed until Monday at the earliest."

Scarlett looked around the shop and wondered if she'd be forced to create any atrocious updos on other unsuspecting teens. But if she could get a place to stay, it might be worth it.

"I'd offer you my guest bedroom, but I live out in the country, and since you don't have a car, that wouldn't be practical. At the salon, you'd be almost across the street from Claude's garage. This building had an apartment in the back many years ago, so there's a full bathroom, and we have a sofa sleeper in the back room. There's a café and a burger place nearby."

"Sounds good. Do you have more appointments this afternoon?"

"Hon, we've got four more coming in and I'm about dead on my feet. Venetia is probably worn to a nub, too, aren't you, Venetia? We had a part-time stylist, but she up and moved to Dallas with her boyfriend. We could use some help."

"If you'll try to get in touch with Mr. McCaskie, I'll be glad to help out. If on the off chance he can get my car fixed, I'll head out later. Either way, I should be able to handle at least two clients."

"That's real good news." Clarissa swept the vinyl cape off the teen. "You're all finished. I'll ring you up, Shawna, and then I'll make the call out to the school."

Scarlett smiled. "That would be great. Thank you, Clarissa." She was glad to trade a few shampoos, sets and styles for a place to stay—if she got stuck in Brody's Crossing for a couple of nights.

Come Monday, though, she was having her car repaired and getting back on the road to L.A.—come hell, high water or Christmas parades.

LATER THAT DAY, Scarlett stood on the front steps of Clarissa's House of Style and watched the Brody's Crossing Christmas parade pass by. So far she'd seen little girls in red tights and sequined leotards twirling their batons; cute little cowboys leading saddled pinto ponies; the high school marching band belting out a stirring rendition of "God Rest Ye Merry Gentlemen"; and a beautiful vintage Thunderbird with the mayor of Brody's Crossing, a surprisingly young, pretty blonde who waved like a beauty queen. She'd probably been a holiday princess a few years back, Scarlett theorized as she huddled in her hoodie.

And now, the holiday princess float came into view, pulled by a man in a Santa suit driving the McCaskie's Service Station tow truck. That must be Claude, former Santa and absent mechanic. Darn him for being so civic minded. Her poor car was dead and Claude didn't care.

Scarlett shook her head to clear the negative thoughts. The float appeared to be a flatbed trailer of some type wrapped in white paper and fluffy imitation snow. Blue snowflakes and hand-painted candies adorned the sides.

Above, the princesses waved and smiled to the crowd lining the street, their fake-fur-trimmed white dresses blowing in the breeze. There was even a hint of sparkly blue eyeshadow.

Scarlett smiled and waved at Ashley Desmond, whose hair she'd worked on this afternoon. She looked wonderful in her loosely twisted curls. Ashley smiled back, and Scarlett hugged her arms around herself, pleased that although she was stranded in middle America, she'd made a small difference today.

At least Ashley appeared age-appropriate, in a style suited for her face and stature. She had her own "look," which was just about the most important asset a teenage girl could possess. After all, not everyone was the same, inside and out.

Scarlett wished her parents and siblings understood her point of view, but they thought everyone should be satisfied to model their virtues—namely, success, stability and respectability.

Well, she didn't want to be a banker or a doctor or a lawyer, then marry well, produce two or three children on a timetable, and live in the suburbs. She wanted to see the world, meet interesting *individuals* and be appreciated for her talent with hair.

As the holiday princess float moved slowly down the street, Scarlett hoped the teenager would pursue her own dreams, wherever they led her. Even if you sometimes landed halfway to where you were going.

ON SUNDAY AFTERNOON, after Scarlett had slept as long as possible on the slightly lumpy sofa bed in the back room of the salon, Clarissa surprised her. The cheerful blonde bustled into the shop, bringing some cold wind and a whiff of the season. Someone must be cutting evergreen branches, Scarlett thought, as Clarissa placed her purse on the counter.

"I'm going to the drugstore down in Graham, so I thought I'd see if you wanted to get out."

"I might need some things, depending on how long I'm going to be here."

"I imagine it's going to be a few days, and I don't mind saying, I'm glad. I'm really happy for your help, Scarlett."

A feeling of warmth flowed through her, but then reality hit. Scarlett didn't want to feel wanted here in Texas. That was the whole point of leaving Georgia—she needed to get to L.A. She'd come to the realization that even if Claude towed her car later today, it wouldn't be fixed immediately.

"Let me get my shoes on and fluff my hair, and I'll be ready to go."

Clarissa drove them to Graham, where they shopped at a chain drugstore. Graham was quite a bit larger than Brody's Crossing.

"Why don't you come to the community center with me?" Clarissa asked as they drove back to town. "We're putting together some gift bags for the children's Christmas party next Saturday."

"Oh, I don't think—"

"We'd love the help."

Scarlett didn't want to seem ungrateful for the trade-off of the free room and even the trip to the store, but she didn't want to get pulled into the activities of the town, even if the idea of spending time with other people was far more appealing than sitting alone. Today it would be gift baskets, then tomorrow something else, until she was committed to serving as Santa's elf on Christmas Eve!

"I really appreciate it, Clarissa, but I'll pass. I...I won't be here long enough to get involved."

Clarissa seemed surprised, glancing away from the road just a moment. Then she said, "Well, if you don't want to, that's okay. I just thought you might rather be over there than all by yourself."

"I'll catch up on my reading. And if you need anything done at the shop—inventory, cleaning, stocking—just let me know."

"Oh, we're fine. If you change your mind, the community center is just two blocks away. Ask anyone for directions."

"Sure." But Scarlett knew she wasn't going to the center on Sunday afternoon. Doing hair was one thing, but packing gift baskets was way too friendly for someone just passing through.

"I WANT TO SUE THAT NEW hairdresser at Clarissa's House of Style," the voice coming from the reception area insisted. "That red-haired, young, weird-looking one that just got into town." The rather unpleasant, strident tones were directed at James's mother, who worked part-time as his receptionist.

"What happened, Delores? I didn't know Clarissa had hired a new hairdresser," James heard his mother ask.

"She's a menace! This was the first time Ashley was a holiday princess, and her parade was ruined!"

"Ruined? That's just terrible."

Don't encourage her, Mom, James thought as he pushed away from his desk and walked toward the reception area. His mother was too sympathetic to be a good screener, but she had a big heart and people did trust her. The problem was that a few of the citizens of Brody's Crossing had become a bit lawsuit crazy since he'd moved his practice back home last year.

Especially whenever one of the television network "in-depth" reports featured some evil-doing, money-hungry, corporate giant who was out to get the little guy. Last week Myra Hammer had wanted to sue the grocery for selling her bruised bananas. The week before, Sam Gibson had insisted that he should sue the used car dealer in Graham because the pickup he'd just bought had a blowout, so obviously the tire was defective.

The citizens of Brody's Crossing did not need encouragement in the lawsuit department.

"Hello, Mrs. Desmond." Demanding Desmond. That's what everyone called her behind her back. Not him, but he'd heard waitresses, clerks and other workers complain. So far, though, no one had tried to sue *her* for unreasonable demands or poor tips. "What's the problem?"

"As I was telling your mother, that new red-haired hairdresser at Clarissa's ruined my daughter's hair for the holiday princess float and lunch at the community center."

"When you say ruined, do you mean permanently?"

"No! But you know how important the parade is. All the girls wear upsweeps with those little rhinestone clips, and they do their makeup to match. Why, they all look so pretty up there on the float."

James sighed. He remembered how his high school girlfriend, Jennifer Hopkins, had been a holiday princess. She was married now with two children and he…wasn't. "Do you have photos or any other proof?"

"I certainly do! They're all right here, in that disposable digital camera I bought at the CVS in Graham."

"Why don't we wait until you get those photos developed, then we can talk?"

"Just look at them in the little window. You can see clear as day that Ashley's hair is not only inappropriate for a princess float, but is just too trendy for us. Why, it looks like something out of one of those Hollywood Grammys or Oscars or some such nonsense. You *know* how strange those actresses look."

James repressed a sigh and accepted the camera Mrs. Desmond thrust into his hand. "Turn it on right here," she advised him, and he looked at photo after photo of dear Ashley wearing a fake-fur-trimmed gown. Her hair had been fluffed up and back, in some kind of curls, a style that did stand out among the other girls. Ashley's hair appeared a bit softer around her small face.

"It's different." And maybe better, James thought, but didn't add his editorial comment. He was no expert on current teenage hairstyles. Or teenage girl anything.

"So different that I'm sure everyone was laughing behind her back."

"Did anyone make a comment to you or to her?"

"No, but that doesn't mean they weren't thinking it!"

"Did you speak to Clarissa or the new stylist?"

"No, I did not! I didn't see Ashley's hair until I went to the parade, and by then, the damage was already done. I thought I should talk to you first, to see what my legal options are." Demanding Desmond leaned closer and narrowed her eyes. "I didn't want to do or say anything that might influence my legal rights."

James repressed another sigh. "You can't sue because you didn't like the hairstyle. You need actual damages."

"How about the damage to my daughter's image? She won't even talk about it. That's how upset she is."

"James, why don't you talk to that new hairdresser? Maybe she just doesn't understand what's expected of her."

"Mother, don't you think that's *Clarissa's* job?"

"Well, maybe…"

"Excellent idea!" Mrs. Desmond said. "You go talk to Clarissa and you'll see what I mean."

"I don't think—"

"Yes, that sounds reasonable," his mother interrupted.

He glared at his mom, then said, "Mrs. Desmond, with all due respect, I don't have a dog in this fight."

"Dogs? Who's talking about dogs? This is about hairstyles!"

His point exactly, which apparently he wasn't going to be allowed to make between his mother's inherent sympathy and her hopes for a potential client.

"I was just going to lunch."

"Fine. Then you can stop by Clarissa's on your way over to the Burger Barn."

"Mrs. Desmond, I'm not agreeing to take your case."

"Okay, but once you see this new hairdresser, you'll know exactly what I mean. Her hair is as red as the volunteer fire department's new truck! She's not one of us. I don't know where she's from, but it's not around here, that's for sure."

Which made James wonder what a fire-engine-red-haired, innovative stylist was doing in Brody's Crossing, Texas.

A few minutes later, with Mrs. Desmond gone and his mother nibbling on a tuna salad sandwich at her desk, James grabbed his jacket and headed for the Burger Barn, which was across the street from Clarissa's House of Style. Eat first, ask questions later. He would not be lured into the beauty shop out of curiosity. That type of behavior could get him in trouble—with himself, if not anyone else.

But when he walked by Clarissa's, he glanced into the big picture window. Just to see if they were open and working. He squinted against the bright December sunlight, wondering if his eyes could be trusted.

He stopped on the uneven concrete sidewalk and stared as the petite hairdresser brushed and used a blow dryer on someone older—he couldn't tell who from this angle.

Wow. The newcomer's hair really was as red as the fire truck. Her bright green sweater ended just shy of her belly button, which twinkled with a tiny bit of silver or gold. Her jeans were tight in all the right places. Several long strands of beads swung as she wielded the blow dryer. Overall, she looked as if she were a Christmas elf making mischief inside Clarissa's shop.

He approached the door, all thoughts of burgers gone.

Chapter Two

Scarlett looked up from fighting Myra Hammer's tight perm as the door to the shop opened. Holy schmoly. What was a man—especially a man who looked like this one—doing here? Surely there was a barbershop in Brody's Crossing where the young and preppy got their already neat hair cut. Not that she minded looking at six feet of trim, hunky, thirty-something male, dressed in pressed chinos, a blue plaid button-down shirt and a brown leather jacket. His belt matched his polished boots, and his nails appeared clean and trimmed. She just couldn't imagine what he wanted in the very pink House of Style.

"May I help you?" she asked, since Venetia was in the back mixing up color for her client, and Clarissa was off to the café for lunch with "the girls," as she called her friends.

"You must be the new stylist," the dark-haired hunk said with a smile. "The one who's 'not from around here.'"

"Yep, that would be me."

"I'm James Brody," he said, handing her a card from his jacket pocket. "My office is down the street, across from the bank, next to the little park with the fountain."

"Not that you're doing us much good," Myra Hammer interjected. "Won't even do what we ask you to do."

Scarlett frowned and looked at the card. "An attorney? Sorry, but I don't need an attorney. Now, if you were a mechanic, we could talk business."

"Actually, I was hoping you'd have a moment to speak to me." He looked down at Myra, and Scarlett got the impression he was working to keep his expression neutral. "In private."

"I'm busy now. I'll be finished in ten minutes."

"Maybe," Myra said. "I want my hair with a wave, but no little curls. I can't stand those little curls."

Then why did you get a tight perm? Scarlett felt like asking, but didn't. "Ten to fifteen minutes."

"I can grab a burger and come back in fifteen minutes. Unless you'd like for me to wait and we can get something together. If you haven't eaten yet."

He was asking her out to lunch? How odd. He didn't even know her. "That's nice, but…"

"You might as well go to lunch with him," Myra interjected. "He's rich, powerful and single."

"Now, Myra, you know I'm not getting rich in this town," Brody answered. "And I'm hardly powerful."

"You're a Brody, aren't you?" Myra looked up at Scarlett. "Town's named after his family."

"Oh, I hadn't made the connection."

"That was generations ago. They owned a ranch, like most everyone else around here."

"You could be rich if you'd sued that grocery store. I could have gotten sick on bruised bananas."

"But you didn't, because you had enough sense not to eat the bananas, and therefore we didn't have a case."

"So now I have to eat bad bananas to get my due!"

"I didn't say that," James Brody replied, then sighed.

"And besides, I came in to see… I'm sorry. I don't know your name."

"I forgot to tell you. It's Scarlett."

"Scarlett…?"

"Just Scarlett, unless you're from the licensing board or health department or insist on seeing my license."

"That bad, hmm?"

She nodded. "My mother has a warped sense of humor."

"Sorry to hear that." He shifted from one foot to the other, looking uncomfortable—but why? Because he stood in a beauty salon, or because he'd just asked her out to lunch? "So, Scarlett, do you want to get a burger?"

She could definitely use all the free meals she could get, since her car engine, as the snaggletoothed chicken crate man had prophesized, was "blown." But no, she couldn't have lunch. She had another client coming in after Myra was finished with her wave, no tight curls.

"Sorry, but I can't. I'm booked up until after two o'clock. If you want to talk, I'll work you in."

"Well, if that's the best you can do, I'll accept your offer to see me between appointments," he replied, and added a dimpled smile, which proved just how perfectly preppy—and okay, charming—he really was.

"Just remember you can't trust lawyers," Myra said.

"It's good to see you, too, Myra," Brody replied without the dimple, then gave Scarlett another slight, all-suffering smile. "I'll see you in a few."

"I'll be here." As soon as the door closed behind him, Scarlett wondered just exactly what she'd agreed to do… and if she should have held out for the free lunch.

"Hi," James Brody said, as he walked into the salon fifteen minutes later, on the dot. Scarlett finished putting away styling

products into a rolling cart. She dropped a comb in steriliz-
ing solution and turned to face him. "How was your burger?"

"Same as always. I eat there every day, except Chamber
of Commerce monthly luncheons and the occasional meeting with a client."

Scarlett thought that sounded extremely boring, but she
held her tongue. His eating habits were none of her business. Although he was here, making something *his* business.
But what?

Venetia was working with a client. Since she wasn't
very friendly and probably gossiped like a pro, Scarlett
would rather not talk to James Brody in front of her. "Do
you want to go out back to talk? It's not too chilly today.
At least the cold wind has died down."

"Sure. Lead the way."

She had the feeling he was watching her as they made
their way through the shampoo area, the room with the
lumpy pull-out sofa she currently called home, and out the
back door, where there was a small porch.

She settled into the lawn chair, leaned back, raised her
tired feet to the railing and looked up. "Well, Mr. Lawyer,
what did you need to talk about?"

He leaned against the iron railing next to the two steps
going to the parking area, and folded his arms across his
leather jacket and very nice chest. "Mrs. Desmond came
into my office just before lunch. Apparently you fixed her
daughter Ashley's hair on Saturday."

"Oh, yes. Petite girl with—" Scarlett almost said "big
ears," but stopped herself in time "—brown hair."

"Her mother is upset that Ashley's hair wasn't styled as
usual. Or at least in a style similar to the other girls. She
felt Ashley was damaged by being different."

"What?" Scarlett sat upright and swung her feet to the porch. "Ashley loved her hair!"

"Apparently her mother had different ideas."

"Well, her mother is wrong! That traditional updo isn't right for a teenager. She needed something softer, with a little volume…er, on the sides." *To cover up her big ears, not show them off.*

"I know that you believe you gave her a style that was suitable for her face, but you've got to understand that in small towns, being traditional is often more important."

"That's nonsense. There's no reason these girls should look like little cookie cutter dolls. They should get hairstyles that are appropriate for them."

"Their mothers are paying for the styles, so they have some say in the final product."

"If Ashley's mother thinks an updo would look better on her daughter than that cute twisted-curl style I did, she just doesn't know what she's talking about. You should ignore her."

"I'm not encouraging her to sue—"

"Sue! She should be thanking me!"

"She has a different opinion, and whether you or I agree with her, she's Ashley's mother and lives in this town. She feels her daughter was harmed."

"I can't believe this! I'm telling you that Ashley loved her hair. You can ask Clarissa."

"I haven't talked to Clarissa, and neither did Mrs. Desmond, apparently. She came to my office earlier and asked me to talk to you."

"Well, that's ridiculous!"

"I'm just saying that sometime between Ashley leaving the salon and Monday morning, Mrs. Desmond decided to see an attorney. Now, as I said, I didn't encourage her."

"Am I supposed to be grateful for that?"

"Look, if she comes around, just tell her you're sorry you didn't fix her daughter's hair as she was expecting it to be fixed."

"I will not apologize for styling that girl's hair in a flattering, appropriate manner."

"Okay, then, but you might expect complaints about these unfamiliar styles. People might thing they're too… mature."

"That's absurd." Scarlett picked up one of the magazines and turned to a section on teen styles. "Look at these! I didn't do anything near this edgy or dramatic." She shoved the magazine at him.

He thumbed through several pages and raised his eyebrows. He was so well groomed that she couldn't even criticize his brows, skin care or even his hair—although the style was kind of boring with a side part, and just long enough to start to curl at the nape of his neck.

"These are as you say, more dramatic than what you did, but that won't necessarily satisfy Mrs. Desmond."

Scarlett grabbed the magazine and put it back on the little table next to the chair. "I won't be around long enough to care. As soon as my car is repaired, I'm out of here."

James Brody, attorney at law, shrugged. "That might be best."

"Hey, who elected you hairstyle sheriff? This is the twenty-first century. You can't run me out of town!"

He frowned. "I'm just pointing out your best option."

She stepped closer and pointed her own finger at him, nearly jabbing him in the chest—which she didn't actually touch because he might have her arrested for assault. "Listen, I don't need to be told I don't belong here. If you want to be useful, get Claude McCaskie to find the parts he needs to repair my car. I'll be out of here faster than you can say 'lawsuit.'"

"I didn't come down here in any official capacity, and I'm not getting in the middle of the fight."

"Oh, you put yourself in the middle, bub."

His eyes narrowed. "Don't call me bub."

"What are you going to do—sue me?"

He leaned closer, until they were nearly eye to eye. "I might just take Mrs. Desmond's case, at which point I'd have you held over for a trial."

Scarlett's eyes narrowed. If she could, she would have blown smoke and fire from her nose. "You wouldn't dare."

"Don't provoke me."

"You're the one who came down here and threatened me!"

She watched anger and frustration war on his face. Granted, it was a handsome face, but as her Southern belle grandmother used to say, "Pretty is as pretty does." Right now he didn't seem so much like a pretty boy as he did a small-town ogre. What nerve, to come in here and tell her she didn't know how to fix hair, then threaten to keep her here with bogus charges!

"I came here to deflect a possible issue for you. I can see you're not going to cooperate, so I'll be going. Don't be surprised if you get more complaints."

"I never let the criticism of small minds bother me."

"We'll see. I guess that depends on how long you're here and whether Clarissa decides to support you." He turned and stormed down the two steps to the gravel parking space behind the salon, and disappeared around the side of the city hall office building.

Scarlett slumped against the wall. Where would she stay if Clarissa decided she was too much trouble? Damn that car! She should have traded it in on something more reliable years ago, even if her actions did make her seem ungrateful to her parents, who'd given her the clunky monster because it was big, safe and paid for.

That's what happened when you depended on others. That's why she needed to be successful and independent. So she wouldn't have to apologize to the Mrs. Desmonds of the world or defend her actions to her family.

When she was successful, she could express herself and people would actually listen and care. They wouldn't tell her to stop trying to be different. They'd ask her what was next! They'd expect a new, original, bold style.

But right now, she was stuck in a town where mothers expected updos and lawyers threatened to sue over a hairstyle! Unless she hitchhiked to L.A., she'd be here until her car was running again.

Maybe she would have to bite her tongue and play nice, but she wasn't going to like it.

JAMES WAS TOO UPSET by his confrontation with Scarlett to talk to her or about her the rest of the day. He hadn't encountered such a defensive, argumentative person in a long time. Definitely not since moving back home. Although some of the folks around Brody's Crossing could be cranky and opinionated, they didn't actively argue like Scarlett No-last-name. At least, not unless they'd been drinking too much at Dewey's Saloon and Steakhouse. He had a couple of clients who fit that description, but he usually only saw them late on occasional Saturday nights or holiday weekends.

That redheaded stranger was infuriating. He'd tried to be nice and helpful, and she'd gone ballistic on him. Well, maybe not ballistic, but she'd been one step away from poking him in the chest. If she had, he wasn't sure what he would have done. Grabbed her finger and pulled her too close to punch him, that was for sure. The extremely odd and vexing thing was that he'd also had the strangest urge to kiss her while he was at it. Just to shut her up, he told himself. Definitely not for any other reason.

On Tuesday morning, as he worked on a new legal agreement between Troy Crawford and Angelo Ramirez to lease part of the Rocking C, James heard a commotion in the reception area. "It's that new girl at Clarissa's," one of the women said in a whining, shaky tone.

"We didn't tell her to fix our hair this way," another woman said.

James dropped his head in his hands for just a second, then heard his mother reply, "I'm sure James can help you."

"No, I can't," he whispered, but that didn't do any good. He pushed away from his desk and prepared to face the newest hair crisis in Brody's Crossing.

"Oh, James, Maribelle and Ellen want to talk to you," his mother said as he walked up to her desk.

"About their hair," he finished.

The women were obviously sisters. Maybe twins, although he couldn't remember them from growing up here.

"We've worn our hair the same way for…well, for a long time," one of the ladies said. "Here." She thrust forward a photo he recognized as the church directory photographer's work.

"I see," he said. The picture showed a woman frozen in time, with an extremely traditional, tightly curled hairstyle and oversize beige, plastic-framed glasses. It could have been taken last year or thirty years ago.

"That girl said she'd like to try something flattering, and well, since she's from Atlanta on her way to California to work at a fancy salon, we said okay," the other woman said.

"We didn't expect her to do anything really different," the first woman whined.

He looked at their softer waves, the pale blond replacing the slightly blue color in the photo, and the ends kind of feathering along their necklines. He thought they looked pretty good. "Yes, the style is different, but both of you ladies look very nice."

"Why, thank you, young man," the second woman said.

"But we liked our hair. We felt comfortable with it. We're not even sure how to fix it now. And what are we going to do with all our temporary rinses that we'd stocked up on when the drugstore in Olney went out of business? We must have two years worth of Fanciful!"

James didn't know rinse from wash, and wasn't about to ask. He took a deep breath before telling them they should talk to Clarissa.

Before he could speak, the whiney one added, "We talked to Mrs. Desmond and she said we should talk to you. If we could get enough people, we could file a class action lawsuit and get a lot of money."

James shook his head. "Ladies, there is no basis for a class action lawsuit, where you would need to have suffered actual losses from a defective product or fraudulent contract or claim. You can't sue a hairdresser because you don't like your hairstyle. If you were unhappy, you should have refused to pay for the service."

"That just seems so rude, don't you think, Ellen?"

"Yes. We didn't want to be rude, even though she is awfully different, with that red hair and those wild clothes." The one who must be Maribelle leaned close to his mother and added, "She has one of those pierced belly buttons. That would be so painful! And can you imagine how many times it would get snagged on your clothes?"

James closed his eyes at the image of Scarlett's belly button ring getting snagged on *his* clothes. On his zipper… He did not need this complication. "Please, go talk to Clarissa. I'm sure she can straighten this out."

"Oh, we can't talk to Clarissa. She lives here."

He felt as if his head were about to explode. "I've already talked to Scarlett, and she's leaving as soon as her car is repaired. That could be any day."

"But what about the lawsuit?"

"There is no lawsuit!"

"James, really, you don't need to yell," his mother reminded him. "It's not professional."

"I'm sorry, but this controversy over the new stylist has gotten out of hand." Not that he would mind getting his hands on Scarlett, just to shake her up, of course. Not for any other reason.

"I think you should talk to her again," his mother said, before he could tell her not to get involved.

"I don't think that's a good idea."

"But you're so good at working out these problems."

"We want you to see if there are other people who want to get in on this class action thing."

"There is no class action lawsuit!"

"James, you're yelling again."

He closed his eyes and nodded. "Yes, I'm sorry. If I promise to speak to Scarlett and Clarissa, will you promise me that you'll wait to do anything? No talking to anyone else, and Mrs. Desmond especially?"

"Oh, all right. We always did like Clarissa," Ellen said, her tone one of resignation.

"But we aren't so sure about our hair," Maribelle added in her whiney voice.

"I'll go see them today. Just—" He held up his hand in

what was probably a futile gesture to keep them silent. "Just don't talk to anyone about your hair unless they compliment you, and then you can say, 'Thank you.'"

As soon as the ladies left and he admonished his mother *one more time* not to encourage potential clients who wanted to sue businesses in or around Brody's Crossing, he called Clarissa Bryant. A few minutes later, he told his mother he was going out for a while.

With heavy steps and a sense of foreboding, he walked the block or so to his hair appointment with Scarlett, recently of Atlanta, on her way to California, who really didn't like him all that much. He was beginning to feel a little bit sorry for the temporary, temperamental stylist. And for himself, for being in the middle of a hair crisis.

"YOU'RE MY ELEVEN O'CLOCK?" Scarlett asked as she stared, openmouthed, at James Brody. He slipped out of his jacket and hung it on the rack.

"I am," he said, easing into her chair. "I thought I'd see what look you might choose for me, given you have such strong opinions about the right style for everyone else." He crossed his hands over his flat stomach and gave her a smarmy lawyer smile. "You are capable of cutting men's hair, aren't you?"

"Perfectly capable," she replied, snapping open a black cape while she gritted her teeth. So now he was tempting her to run her fingers through his thick, dark brown hair? Fine. She was a professional.

"Telling you this probably isn't a good idea," he said as she picked up a razor, "but I had two more visitors to my office."

She tested the sharpness of the blade with her finger,

then looked at him through her lashes. "Really? More irate mothers with poor taste in hair and clothes?"

He shifted in the chair as he watched her handle the implement. "No. Irate grandmothers."

"Who?" she asked, putting the razor down and picking up a spray bottle. She misted his hair with water.

"Maribelle and Ellen. Twins or close to it. Formerly with steel-blue curls."

"Ah yes, I remember them well." She bit the bullet and sank her fingers into his hair, all the way to the scalp. He was warm and he smelled really good, like crisp soap and clean male. She spent an extra moment savoring the feel of his strong, healthy hair. When she finished working the water through, she looked at him in the mirror. His hair was clumped into spikes around his well-shaped head. He had the kind of bone structure and features that could pull off almost any style.

"Are you ready to get started?"

"Oh, sure." She made her decision, seeing his style in the lay of his hair, the amount of curl and body. "What about Maribelle and Ellen?"

"They were sort of complaining. They seemed distressed that their style and color were different."

"They were happy when they left. Sort of." She pulled his hair between her fingers, angled away from his head, and ran the razor along the ends.

"I promised them I'd talk to you." He sighed, then said, "Actually, I told my mother I'd talk to you."

"Aren't you a little old to be reporting to your mommy?" She had to distance herself, because he was entirely too appealing on a physical level.

"She works for me. And I don't *report* to her."

"Whatever. Why do these supposedly dissatisfied customers keep coming to you rather than mentioning to me or Clarissa that they're unhappy with their hair?"

"They told me that withholding payment or talking to Clarissa seemed rude. I told them there was no basis for a class action lawsuit, but I have a theory."

Class action lawsuit! As if she were a faulty heater! She worked her way up to the crown of his head and forced herself to relax. "What's your theory about this lawsuit that shouldn't even be considered?"

"Don't worry. No one is filing a lawsuit. However, ever since I returned to Brody's Crossing last year, I've had a steady stream of folks wanting to sue. There must be some pent-up legal needs in town, because I've had some wild requests."

Scarlett took a deep breath and decided to ignore talk of lawsuits, focusing instead on the information he'd revealed about himself. "Where did you return from?"

"Fort Worth."

"That's not very far." She'd almost gone through Fort Worth when she'd taken that wrong turn in Dallas.

"Not in miles, but it is in culture."

"Were you a lawyer there?"

"Yes, corporate law."

She couldn't imagine a more boring profession. Who would choose that kind of work when they could be talking to real people all day? Of course, being a corporate attorney would pay a whole lot more than her stylist salary. Enough that he probably wouldn't be stuck in Brody's Crossing with a huge car repair bill that he couldn't really afford.

"Why did you come back here?"

"I decided that the folks here needed legal representation, whether they made good decisions or not."

"I don't think it's wise to sue someone who makes you look better." She finished her initial razor cut, then used her fingers to pull his hair out from his scalp, eyeing the length of each strand as she did so. She made a few adjustments. Perfect.

"Probably not, but then, I'm not encouraging them."

"And yet you're right in the middle of this would-be controversy." She put down her razor and picked up the styling gel.

"So true." He twisted around to look at the product. "What are you putting in my hair?"

"Something to give it a little body and shape."

"It's not colored, is it?"

"No. It's clear."

"I don't want stiff, blue or purple hair."

He seemed so cautious that she smiled. "Honey, this won't make you stiff."

He stilled, meeting her eyes in the mirror. His were hot. Smoldering. Not the least bit angry. She stared back, suddenly realizing what she'd said to this very attractive, single man. She'd definitely grabbed his attention. This time, she couldn't blame their awareness on an argument.

At least, not yet. She was pretty sure they'd get around to disagreement sooner or later.

"Anyway," she said, breaking eye contact, squeezing a dab into her palm, "you have to trust me. This is good stuff."

"So you say," he replied, settling back in his chair.

She rubbed the gel through his thick, somewhat shorter hair. It felt good. Too good. She was a stylist, for heaven's sake. She shouldn't react this strongly to *hair.*

To distract herself, and keep him from seeing the finished product, she spun the chair around to face the row of old-fashioned bonnet-style hair dryers lined up on the other wall. This time of day, in the middle of the week, they were all empty.

She used the hand-held dryer, shaping his slightly damp strands into a hip style, something a successful, thirty-something city dweller might wear. Of course, James Brody was a small-town lawyer, not a big-city stockbroker or advertising executive, but still, she thought he looked good. Okay, more than good. He looked *hot*.

"What are you doing?"

"Don't be impatient. I'll turn you around in a minute. Like I said, trust me."

"This from a woman with bright red spiky hair," he replied.

"Yeah, well, it matches my name."

"I wonder which came first."

"It's a chicken-and-egg kind of thing. I'm Scarlett, through and through, thanks to Logics R6."

"Hmm. I take it that's fire-engine-red hair color?"

"Right." She finished up his hair and didn't say anything else stupid. Before she spun him around, she took a real good look at her work. Yep, star quality. Hollywood worthy. And not just the haircut. "You're done," she said, twirling him toward the mirror.

His eyes widened, then narrowed. However, he didn't frown. He assessed. He tilted. He studied. "Hmm. Different, but I kind of like it."

His hair wasn't smooth like before, and didn't have a part. She'd pulled the short strands forward in a natural style. "Really? I mean, that's great." She unfastened the vinyl cape and swung it away from his big shoulders. She was used to small shoulders. Women, mostly. Not hot, hunky guys. She brushed a few hairs from his yellow shirt.

He paused at her touch, then stood and reached for his wallet. "What do I owe?"

"Um, you'll have to ask Clarissa. I don't know what she charges for men's razor cuts."

He sauntered to the front of the salon. Scarlett followed him with her gaze until she realized Venetia was probably staring. She looked at the other stylist. Yep, staring. Scarlett smiled like she really didn't mean it, and then tried her best to eavesdrop on Clarissa and James.

"Yes, she does a good job, doesn't she?" Clarissa said. "People might be surprised, but I swear, business has picked up in just three days." She leaned closer and said more softly, so that Scarlett could barely hear, "Personally, I think a lot of folks come by out of curiosity, but whatever brings them in is fine with me."

"A few have mentioned that they were…concerned that their hairstyles were different than they were expecting," he said to Clarissa very tactfully.

"Really? No one's said anything to me."

"I've told them to talk to you or Scarlett."

Clarissa patted his arm. "Good advice, as usual."

James paid what he owed, then handed over some more money. A tip? After leaning close and saying something that made Clarissa laugh, he turned. Scarlett looked away and started sweeping up his dark, shorn hair.

"So, like a lot of your clients, I look different," he said to her, hesitating near her station.

"I think you look great. I mean, better."

"I'm getting used to it." He bent a little to glance in the mirror, raking a hand through his hair before continuing. "I don't look much like a corporate lawyer."

No, he looked like the hunky doctor on the TV show about people stranded on an island, only he needed a few days' worth of beard and a torn T-shirt. "That's because you're not a corporate lawyer anymore. You're *the* Brody's

Crossing lawyer, apparently now specializing in controversial hairstyles."

"You're right." He smiled at her, then paused before saying, "I realize that we got off to a bad start. Could I take you to dinner to make up for it?"

"Dinner?"

"The meal most of us eat at night."

"I know what it means, but I thought I'm supposed to be the enemy. I'm not sure why you'd want to be seen with me in public." She narrowed her eyes and watched him. "You are talking about a real restaurant, right? Not going to your apartment or your mother's?"

"Dinner in public at Dewey's, you and me, no mother. Why don't I pick you up around six? And where are you staying?"

"Right here," she said, pointing to the rear of the salon. "Back room sofa. Home sweet home." Until she was no longer stranded in Texas.

Chapter Three

"So, tell me how you came to be stuck in Brody's Crossing," James asked once they'd been seated in a relatively quiet corner of Dewey's. The high backs of the dark vinyl booth enfolded them and kept the country-and-western music from interfering with conversation.

Scarlett fiddled with her paper napkin and rearranged the flatware on the table, then said, "It's simple. I was on my way to California, took a wrong turn in Dallas, ended up going a different way to the I-40, and then my aging Benz broke down."

"How bad is it?"

"Claude pulled the engine and is getting estimates on parts, but he thinks it's going to be bad. Real bad. Something about a cracked piston ring."

"That does sound bad."

"Honestly, I didn't plan to spend all my money on that car. My parents gave it to me ten years ago." She shrugged. "I guess I thought it would just keep going forever. I probably should have traded it in, but I never got around to it, and they kept telling me how safe it is."

"So, what's waiting for you in California?" *Boyfriend?* he wondered. She wasn't wearing an engagement ring or anything similar. As a matter of fact, she wore lots of rings, but they all looked…casual. Like costume jewelry rather than serious jewels. Her manner of dress was also casual— very California.

"A great opportunity. I'm starting an internship in January at a very prestigious salon in L.A. Really, it's a once-in-a-lifetime chance."

She seemed so excited about her new job, and granted, working in a prestigious salon seemed like a big goal. Scarlett—whatever her real name was—fairly radiated energy. "Sounds important for you to get there."

"Yes, it is. I met Diego, the owner, at a hair show in Atlanta. We hit it off, basically because I knew all the great places to shop and people watch, which is his specialty. Anyway, we had a good time, he liked my work and he offered me an internship at his salon. You would not believe the client list! He does hair for some of the top movers and shakers in town."

As James wondered why he was mildly jealous of the people-watching Diego, Twila, who was the cousin of his eleventh-grade girlfriend, came and took their drink orders. James had a beer, and instead of something sophisticated, urbane and expensive, Scarlett ordered a diet soft drink. "Tell me you're old enough to drink," he teased when the waitress left.

She laughed, a hearty, real laugh that warmed him. "Yes, I've been old enough for oh, about seven years now. I'm just not much of a drinker."

"Twenty-eight is young."

"And you're what, ancient?"

He shrugged. "No, just feels that way sometimes. I'm thirty-three, divorced, and you know this is my hometown. My mother works for me part-time in my law office."

"Working with a relative seems as if it could be a real disaster. You must have a good relationship."

As he wondered if Scarlett was thinking of her own family, he fiddled with his knife and fork. "We do. She got bored sitting around what's left of the family ranch. She and my dad sold off most of the acreage when he retired."

"Ah, yes. The Brodys of Brody's Crossing."

"Well, that was in the late 1800s. My mother and father worked for a living. She's a real people person. She and I both agreed that working for me would be good. However, sometimes she's a little too enthusiastic about getting me clients."

"I guess I should be glad you're not anxious to pursue bad-hair grievances."

"Well, that's a boon for me, at least. I thought you might still be angry."

"No, I got over that pretty quick. Besides, you're buying me a meal. And offering something new to do. Believe me, sitting around the back room of the House of Style all night is not my idea of a rocking good time. Clarissa doesn't even have a TV, and I'm really getting tired of easy listening, classic rock and country, country, country on the radio."

That did sound pretty boring. "I'm glad I can be a diversion."

"I didn't mean that's all you are," she quickly added.

"I didn't take it that way. I didn't realize how 'stuck' you really are. I can't imagine not having a car to get where you want to go."

She nodded. "I need to find an apartment and get settled in L.A. before Christmas."

"I know you want to go to California, but it must be hard being away from your family during the holidays." How many people could give up Christmas in order to start over in a strange town? That had to be difficult.

"Oh, not as much as you might expect," she said, spreading her paper napkin on her lap. "I have a sister and a brother to fill in the gap, plus my sister-in-law is pregnant. And trust me, the parents are much happier to talk about the doctor, the accountant and the upcoming grandchild than they are talking about the 'hairdresser.'"

"But they're your family! Do you really think they're disappointed in you?"

She shrugged. "I do. I'm a *hairdresser*—they can't remember that I'm a *stylist*—in a perfect suburban family of overachievers. It's not something they brag about."

What could he say to that? James had a hard time imagining a family that wasn't supportive, because his parents had always been loving, even when he'd done some rather stupid things in high school. Darn his best friend, Wyatt. That boy could have talked a saint into sinning! But when Wyatt had left for Stanford, James had gone to UT Austin and cleaned up his act to get into law school.

He understood goals, which Scarlett had, even if the goal wasn't something her parents considered important.

"Do you like Atlanta?" he asked.

She shrugged again. "It's okay. It's kind of traditional, you know?"

James was saved from asking what was so wrong with tradition as Twila came to take their dinner orders. "What can I get you?" she asked.

Scarlett folded her menu. "I'll have the meat loaf with mashed potatoes and gravy, green beans, and a salad with ranch. Oh, and two dinner rolls, please."

James smiled, thinking of her petite figure and her big appetite. "I'll have the sirloin, medium, baked potato, and a salad with blue cheese." He looked at Scarlett. "Are you sure you don't want a steak?"

"No, I have a real craving for meat loaf tonight."

"Comfort food?"

She rearranged her knife and fork again. "Something like that."

SCARLETT LEANED BACK against the leather seat of James's sporty red SUV. She'd been surprised earlier that his vehicle was red, but hadn't made any snappy remarks. She was trying to be on her best behavior, since the man had bought her a meal, and she was way too bored to go back to the salon early if she insulted him accidentally.

He'd told her that he'd really just wanted to make up for making her angry, for letting their conversation in back of the salon get out of hand. The way she remembered it, she'd been the one who'd accelerated that conflict, but he had made her angry with what he saw as a reasonable suggestion. She still didn't see why he'd put himself in the middle of the hair wars between her and her clients.

She sighed, and didn't realize he'd heard until he asked, "Are you okay?"

"Sure. I'm just thinking." She sat up straighter. "Hey, look at those Christmas lights! That's really cool." A whole herd of white-light reindeer stood on a small lawn where all the bushes and trees sported multicolored lights.

"You probably haven't seen any of our Christmas lights, have you? Would you like to drive around a little?"

"That would be great!" She definitely wasn't ready to face another boring night of country-and-western Christmas tunes on the FM radio at the salon.

James turned left off the road that led downtown from Dewey's, onto a smaller residential street. "Lots of families around here go all-out to decorate their homes for the holidays. Sometimes you can see the lights from hundreds of yards away, when the houses sit far back from the road."

He cruised slowly down the street, which was lined with normal-size yards and houses.

"I love the icicle lights that hang down from the eaves and gutters," she said, leaning close to the window. Since the temperature was fairly mild, her breath barely made a frosty spot on the glass.

When she was a little girl, she would breathe on the glass on purpose and write with her finger. Her parents were not amused, since they'd paid someone to wash the car and clean the interior. She got in trouble even after she started writing her sister's name on the glass, which apparently didn't fool anyone, since her sister was too much of a goody-two-shoes to deface clean car windows.

"Oh, look, multicolored icicle lights. I like those."

"You would," James said.

She heard the smile in his voice and glanced at him. His profile was nearly as perfect as his face. His hair still looked adorably ruffled, as if he'd rolled out of bed and run his fingers through it.

Which, of course, hadn't been her intention when she'd cut it earlier. Had it?

"Why did you say that? Do you know me so well already?"

"I know that the traditional icicle lights are white, so naturally you'd like the most colorful ones. Tell me if I'm wrong."

She settled back against the seat. "No, you're right. I'm a rebel without a cause."

"Maybe you don't have a cause, but you have a goal, and that's just as important."

She sat up a little straighter. "I suppose you're right! Even if other people don't understand or agree with me, it's my goal, and darn it, I will get to California."

"I never doubted it for a second. And," he said, slowing the car and looking over at her, "I really wouldn't have filed a lawsuit and kept you in town. I only said that because you…well, you irritated me for a moment."

"I never seriously thought you would. Oh, you might think about it. You might even mentally plan the whole thing. But I didn't think you'd go through with it."

"You know me that well?"

She shrugged. "Seems that way. Now, let's find some more Christmas lights before they roll up the sidewalks in this town."

James laughed and turned left at the end of the street. Scarlett smiled into the darkness, blew on the glass and wrote his initials with her finger. However, unlike when she was just a kid, she didn't draw a heart around them. That would be just too stupid, since in a couple of days she'd be out of here.

But she wanted to…

ON WEDNESDAY AFTERNOON Claude McCaskie called and asked Clarissa if Scarlett could walk over to the service station. Since she didn't have any customers then, Scarlett skedaddled out the door, hoping like heck that the man would have good news.

"Tell me you've found the parts," she said, breathless from nearly-jogging in her high-heeled boots.

"Nope," Claude replied. "The places I usually get reasonably priced parts from in Fort Worth don't have any piston rings for that engine, and I'm runnin' out of options."

"No! I really need to get my car fixed."

Claude shook his head. "I've got one more place to check in Dallas. Now, the problem is, the rings they get might be really used, if you get my drift."

"I know we were trying to save money. That's the only way I can afford the repairs."

"Just so you know. But I don't want to leave you stranded again beside the highway. There might not be another town so close by."

That was true. She was nearly to the most desolate part of her trip, out through the uninhabited Wild West lands of New Mexico and Arizona. "Could you try? Maybe they can find slightly used parts."

"Missy, ain't nothin' slightly used on an old engine like this unless it was wrecked right off the bat. But I'm tryin'."

"I appreciate it, Claude," she answered, trying not to seem too dejected.

"If I can't find them parts, do you want me to look into new ones? It's gonna cost a lot more, but they'd be a lot more reliable."

Scarlett sighed. "Get me a price and I'll see what I can afford."

"You could always see what you'd get for junk."

"Junk?"

"For the Mercedes. At the junkyard or the auction."

She felt her eyes widen and the breath leave her lungs. Just for a moment. "No, I can't do that." Not yet. The Benz was still in good shape. It was just those pesky piston rings. Surely people didn't trash their perfectly good cars because of something so small.

So darn hard to find!

Besides, the car was her link to her past. Okay, to her family. They'd given it to her. It didn't seem right to practically throw it away.

"'Course, we could try for a new engine. Well, not new, but with less miles. New to this car."

"Oh, that's an idea. How much is a new engine?"

"Probably about the same as new rings, but I 'spect we'd be able to *find* an engine. I can get some prices."

"Thanks, Claude. Call me when you have news. You know where I'll be."

"I surely do," he replied with an irritating chuckle.

Scarlett left the service station and pulled her hoodie close around her. The wind was picking up again, but it wasn't too cold. The sun shone on the silver tinsel and candy canes along the main street, pulling her eye toward the two-story building on the next block. The one next to the little park, which she hadn't visited. Yet.

With resolve to get out of her funky mood, she set off for downtown Brody's Crossing. Maybe she should visit a park. Or a lawyer who had an office right beside one.

JAMES LOOKED UP FROM reading a brief when his door opened, then closed. He wasn't expecting anyone. He hoped no one had any more bad-hair cases.

"Hello?"

He recognized Scarlett's voice and pushed back from his desk immediately. "In here."

She appeared at the doorway to his office, her cheeks nearly as red as her hair. She seemed even more disheveled than usual, as if she'd battled the wind all the way down the street.

"You look cold. Can I make you some coffee?"

"Do you have hot chocolate?" she asked, blowing into cupped hands.

"Let's check." He walked toward her and she scooted back, out of the doorway, so he could pass. She obviously didn't want to make contact.

He felt her presence as he hunkered down in front of the cabinet where the coffeemaker and microwave perched next to the mini-refrigerator. "Looks like you're in luck. My mother keeps the cabinet well stocked with almost anything a client or potential client would want."

"Great. Clarissa keeps the coffee going all day, and I've had enough to keep me awake until January."

James chuckled as he filled the coffee carafe at the small sink. "I think this hot water will be okay for the hot chocolate."

"Or I could make it in the microwave. I'm not picky as long as I get warmed up." Scarlett rubbed her hands together as if emphasizing her words. "I wish I was already in California."

He didn't say anything, and she must have understood how her statement sounded, because she added, "Oh, not that I'm not enjoying your company, but weatherwise…"

"I understand. It's difficult for a small Texas town to compete with sun and surf. Not to mention mud slides, brush fires and earthquakes."

"Very funny. Those are rare occurrences."

"Here's some hot chocolate to warm you until you can get past those burning hills to the sunny beaches."

"You're a bundle of joy, aren't you? Just what I needed to cheer me up after talking to Claude McCaskie." She accepted the white mug, wrapping it in her slender hands with the bright red nail polish on her fairly short nails. "But thanks for the hot chocolate."

"I'm just joking with you." Sort of. He wasn't a big fan of California. He'd gone to a legal conference out there and had ended up stuck in traffic, confined to his hotel due to dangerous smoke in the air, and then had a flight delay after a small earthquake. Of course, the beach had been spectacular. Not to mention the beautiful, tanned California girls in bikinis. "Did Claude have some news about your car repairs?"

"No real news," Scarlett said with a sigh. She updated James on the conversation she'd just had with the mechanic, even the part about getting rid of the Benz.

"So he mentioned junking it?"

She shook her head. "I don't want to talk about it." She turned away and walked around the office. "It's cozy in here. I like the exposed brick wall."

"I do, too. This is one of the oldest brick buildings in town, built in the 1920s. Many of the original, frame structures burned after a particularly civic minded prohibitionist set fire to the local honky-tonk."

"Hmm, sounds like they could have used a good lawyer."

"Maybe. I'm not sure if there was one back then. Come to think of it, my predecessor could have been practicing then. He was pretty old when he passed on last year."

"Is that when you moved back to town?"

"My parents became ill. My father first, and then my mother, from taking care of him. I knew I needed to move back here, even with their friends in town helping out. I was married at the time, and things got complicated."

"Your wife didn't want to move?"

"That's right. How did you know?"

"I'm a stylist. Women tell me things. One of the biggest stresses in a marriage is when one of the spouses either gets transferred or decides to move. They think the other one will go along, but find out their partner doesn't feel the same way. I see it from both sides—women who want to transfer and expect their husbands to understand, and women who are in peril of being uprooted when their husbands take a new job."

"I thought Babs and I agreed on the importance of family, and had discussed the advantages of raising a family in the country."

"Your wife was named Babs?"

"That was her nickname."

"Hmm."

"What does that mean?"

"Nothing," Scarlett replied, setting her empty mug down in the sink. "You know, discussing the relative merits of country versus city life is a lot different than actually moving."

"I found that out the hard way."

"Do you miss her?"

"Not like I should have if we were meant to stay together. Sometimes I think I miss being married, but no, I don't miss her very much at all." Especially after the rather nasty things she'd told him during the divorce. Damn it, he was not a boring country hick. He liked his roots in ranching country. His values came from his community and his family, and he wasn't ashamed of either.

"Speaking of country," Scarlett said, placing her hands in the back pockets of her jeans. Her movements drew his attention to the partially unzipped hooded sweatshirt and bright green T-shirt that stretched over her breasts. When he looked up, he saw amusement in her eyes. He'd been caught staring, and wondered if he should grin or apologize.

"I'd really like to see some of the ranches and land around here," she said with humor in her voice. "And since I don't have a car, I'm out of luck. Could I tempt you to play hooky from the office this afternoon?"

He took a deep breath. Could he just close up the office and drive around the countryside with Scarlett No-last-name? He didn't have any appointments, but a potential client might stop by, or someone could need advice. Then there was that legal brief of a case he might be involved with before long, down at the county courthouse in Graham.

And then there was the thought of spending time with

Scarlett. In just two days she'd made him ignore his good intentions twice—once to go into the salon instead of eating lunch first, then his impromptu invitation to dinner. Not to mention the way she'd raised his temper.

"That is, if your mommy doesn't mind," Scarlett added, and that sealed the deal.

He grabbed a sheet of paper, quickly wrote a note, and snatched a piece of tape off the dispenser on the reception desk. Then he checked to make sure the answering machine was on and that his cell phone was clipped to his waist. If anyone called, they'd get a recording that listed his mobile number. He might be playing hooky, but he did have a little sense left.

"Let's go," he said, switching off the lights.

Chapter Four

Sunlight streamed through the windshield and side windows of James's red SUV as he drove out of town toward the gentle hills surrounding Brody's Crossing. Scarlett snuggled into the leather seat and enjoyed the feeling of warmth and security. He was a good driver and she felt lulled into safety by his presence. She really didn't care where they were headed as long as it wasn't back to Clarissa's House of Style or McCaskie's Service Station.

"Would you like to see the Brody family ranch?"

"Sure. Do you still raise cattle?"

"No. My dad is retired, but they keep a few pets. My mother got some goats from someone new in town, Raven York. She's originally from New Hampshire, so I guess you could say that she's the previous 'not from around here' newcomer. She married into another local ranching family, the Crawfords. Her husband, Troy, is a client of mine."

"I haven't met her yet."

"She eats lunch with Clarissa and her group at the café sometimes. You should meet her. She's very much into natural foods and recycling and all that."

"I haven't gotten into that yet. Maybe once I'm in L.A."

James chuckled. "You're going to *plan* on becoming environmentally aware?"

Scarlett shrugged. "I don't know. I haven't thought much about it. But that kind of thing is popular in California."

"How about what you think? What you believe in?"

"I believe it's important to be eco friendly. I just haven't thought about it much."

"What about your family?"

"My mother recycles newspapers, glass and plastic." When Scarlett lived at home, it was always her job to drag the stuff out to the curb once a week.

"No, I mean, what are they like? Do you think you'll miss them?"

She shrugged. "I guess. Like I told you before, they aren't really excited about my career, so they probably think moving to California is stupid. We sort of agreed not to discuss it."

"I can't imagine not discussing career choices with my family. My mother would be so hurt, and my father would question my motives if I didn't want to talk about it."

"Yeah, well, families are different. Let's just say that mine are happy I can pay my own bills." She paused a moment, then frowned. "Except for my recent setback. At least I'm earning some money and Clarissa is letting me stay at the salon for free."

"She's a nice lady. Very friendly. She gives some of the older ladies on a fixed income a 'special rate' for seniors, and every year for prom, she does lots of hair for free, for the girls who can't afford it."

"She is nice. I'm lucky to have found her."

"She feels the same about you."

Scarlett sat up straighter and looked at James. "She does?"

He nodded. "She told me that business has picked up

and you're the reason. She's glad you're here. I think she likes you, even though the two of you are very different."

"Hmm. I just figured she's friendly to everyone."

"She is, but she feels protective of you, I think. She worries about you."

"I'm fine! Or I will be, as soon as I get my car fixed."

James shook his head. "You don't get it. People around here really care for each other. That's what community means. I found out how much we could depend on our neighbors when my parents needed help, when Mom and Dad didn't want to 'bother' me with their problems. Everyone pitched in to go grocery shopping, make them meals, feed the animals, take my parents to the doctor. I wanted to move back because those are the kind of people I want to be around."

"Even if it cost you your marriage?"

He seemed to contemplate his answer for a moment, then said, "Even then. If Babs didn't understand how important community was to me, if she thought I could continue in that law firm when they obviously didn't care about any of the associates, then she didn't know me at all."

"You know, I grew up in a neighborhood where everyone kept to themselves. I have to admit that I don't get the whole community thing, either."

"If you stay around here, you will."

"That's a nice thought," she replied, settling back in the sun-warmed seat. "But I'm headed west as soon as possible."

"What better time than Christmas to discover how folks really come together to care and help each other?"

"I guess." But she wasn't convinced she'd discover any such thing.

"Here's the ranch," James announced, pulling off the two-lane road onto a long gravel drive. "Ready to meet the folks?"

"No!"

He laughed and stopped the SUV. "If you want to drop in for coffee and cake, we can."

"No, I just wanted to see the countryside. Really, I don't want to inconvenience anyone. Anyone else, I should say, since I did ask you to drive me around."

"You wanted a diversion."

She scrunched up her face. "Well, yeah, but I came to *you*. Doesn't that show how high you rank on the diversion meter?"

James laughed. "I don't mind being your chauffeur. I'm enjoying the afternoon."

"Okay, then, let's keep driving. I'm sure your parents are great and all, but wouldn't they think it's weird that you're bringing me out here to meet them?"

He shrugged. "I don't think so, if I explained the situation to them."

"You'd tell them I made you play hooky from your legal practice? That makes me sound like a terrible person."

"I'm not some perfect angel. I did a lot of stupid things when I was younger. Now I'm very responsible…almost all the time. They'd accept that I wanted to drive you around, show you the ranches and countryside."

"Then your parents are a lot more trusting than mine."

He looked at her intently for a long moment before turning his attention back to the car. With efficiency he backed the SUV onto the grass beside the drive, then reversed their direction. "Okay. We keep driving around. No parents. No coffee, cake and questions."

Scarlett breathed a sigh of relief. "Thanks."

He drove about for another half hour, showing her various ranches and landmarks. They went to the edge of Lake Graham, which was not a pretty sight this time of year. The water was brownish-green, low from the look of the banks, and the grass surrounding the area was winter dry. They didn't stay long, heading back to Brody's Crossing as the sun sank lower in the afternoon sky.

"Thanks again for driving me around. This was great. I feel much more relaxed now."

"You're welcome," James said with a smile that warmed her heart. Not that she should allow any man to warm her heart right now, when she could be leaving in a few days.

They stopped at one of the two lights along Main Street. "You know, we should go out to Dewey's for their Christmas party on Saturday."

"Don't you have a date already?"

"No, I don't."

"I might not be here Saturday."

"Oh, Scarlett, I hate to burst your bubble, but there's no way Claude could get an engine or even a part for your engine and install it that quickly."

"Oh." She felt deflated, suddenly brought back to reality. And then she felt something else—James's fingers on her cheek.

"Hey, it's okay. You'll get to California. You'll get to join Raoul—"

"Diego," she said softly, smiling at James. She suddenly realized their heads were quite close together.

"Whatever. You'll get there," he declared.

She nodded, then they both jumped at the light tap of a horn. They turned and looked behind them.

"Oops," he said, smiling and waving at the four elderly ladies behind him. All of them looked at him curiously, craning their necks to see inside the SUV. He stepped on the gas and continued down Main Street toward his office.

"You know those ladies?"

"Yes, I do," he replied somewhat nervously. "That's my retired English teacher, her sister and friends. They play bridge at least once a week at the community center. And they are very big gossips."

"Oh, then you are so busted."

James pulled into his parking space behind the building, then shrugged. "I don't know what you're talking about. I'm a model citizen."

"And we didn't do anything wrong!"

"I know." He turned off the engine and pivoted toward her. "Scarlett, you are a dangerous woman. I should be reading some boring 'homework,' not cruising around with a pretty girl, getting caught by my former English teacher."

"Homework?"

"It's a case that's coming up in less than two weeks. I'm going to be sitting in for a judge in Graham, which is the county seat. I need to be familiar with the case."

"Wow, a judge. I thought you had to be old, gray and paunchy to be a judge."

"The position is just temporary. I'm not running for judge." He shrugged again. "At least, not now."

"But still, serving even temporarily is an honor, right?"

"The judge I'm subbing for is an old friend of the family. He's one reason I went to law school."

"I'd better not keep you from your homework, then." He was going to be a judge, for goodness sake! She'd only been thinking of herself when she'd enticed him away from his office. "I'd better go."

"Would you like to come in for some more hot chocolate?"

"I can't. I have to…get back to the salon."

"Oh." He reached out and fingered a strand of her hair, as if testing to see if it was real. "Are you sure?"

She was pretty certain she shouldn't be sitting out here

with Mr. Hunky Lawyer. She nodded, not trusting her voice. As she reached for the door, James put his hand on her shoulder.

"You never did tell me that you'd go to the Christmas party at Dewey's Saloon and Steakhouse. It's the event of the season in Brody's Crossing. You can't miss it."

"James, do you think—"

"Yes, I do," he said, leaning close. "As crazy as this seems. Or maybe I'm not thinking at all…." She watched in shock as his lips descended, as his eyelids lowered, as he kissed her.

Only then did she close her own eyes and give in to the feelings he aroused. Oh, yes, aroused. She went from surprised to turned on in a nanosecond. His lips molded over hers, his tongue touched hers and she moaned into his mouth. She wasn't sure how long the kiss lasted, only that she wanted it to go on forever.

When he pulled back, she went with him. Only for a second, but long enough to show how much she liked kissing him. And he knew, darn him. He smiled slowly as he looked into her eyes.

"Was that a yes?"

JAMES WATCHED SCARLETT nearly run from the parking lot, around the side of the building to Main Street. She hadn't given him an answer, which meant he'd need to go back to the salon to see her before Friday. The party was Saturday night, and he planned to attend with her.

He wanted her to see that his hometown was different, that family and friends were important. He wasn't even sure why it was so vital to him to make Scarlett see his point. There was something so sad about her going on her own to California during the holidays. Something so lonely about the way she thought of her place in her family. Could her relatives really not see what a wonderful, vibrant person she was?

He got out of the SUV and entered the back door of the office building, and in minutes was sitting at his desk.

Just as he was before Scarlett walked into his office an hour ago.

Just as he'd done before Scarlett came to town, days ago. Just as he'd be doing after she left town, days from now.

He opened the brief to the page he'd been reading, but his mind wasn't ready to stop thinking about Scarlett yet. The words blurred as he remembered his surprise when he'd touched her hair. He'd expected it to be stiff or sticky. Maybe red-hot. But it wasn't. Her red hair was warm and soft, like her lips.

Maybe he shouldn't take her to Dewey's Christmas party. Maybe he shouldn't have kissed her. But he had, and if he had the opportunity, he would again.

Kiss her and more.

SCARLETT HAD MADE SOME mistakes in her life, but kissing James Brody was right up there at the top of her list. Unfortunately, she hadn't come to that conclusion until she'd hightailed it back to Clarissa's House of Style. She'd blamed her hot cheeks and flushed demeanor on the blustery, sunny day instead of James's kisses and her own poor judgment.

When she walked through the back door, she stopped dead and stared, all thoughts of James temporarily forgotten.

"Oh, Scarlett, I'm so glad you're back," Clarissa said. At least, Scarlett *thought* it was Clarissa. She was dressed in some kind of prairie costume, floor length and fitted to her busty frame. She leaned over and pulled a calico bonnet on over her fluffed, sprayed hair.

"What's going on?"

"We're checking our costumes for the annual Settlers Stroll," Clarissa explained. "I must have gained a few pounds. Either that or my corset sprang a leak," she said with a chuckle.

Venetia emerged from the bathroom in a dress of a similar style, complete with shawl, bustle and bonnet. With her thinner figure and time-worn features, she looked much more like a nineteenth century woman, Scarlett thought.

"We want to get you a costume," Clarissa said, tying the ribbon under her double chin. "The Settlers Stroll is Sunday night, but we shouldn't have any problem. You're so petite that you could wear almost anything."

"Er, I'm not sure I'll be here Sunday night." With any luck, she'd be on the road. Then she wouldn't have to give James an answer about the Christmas party at Dewey's.

"Oh, I talked to Claude when I was hoping to find you over there at the garage. He said there's no way he can get the engine installed before then. So…" Clarissa paused and took a breath, her hand on her ribs—and presumably her tight corset. "You might as well join us. It's a lot of fun."

"I don't have a costume." She didn't have the money to buy one, even if she wanted to.

"Don't worry about that. We have a big inventory of outfits that we store at the community center for everyone who doesn't have their own, courtesy of the McCall family. Of course," Clarissa said, giving Venetia a knowing look, "I imagine it's more that boy of theirs, Wyatt. He's as rich as they come, and probably feels a little guilty for getting a group of teenagers dressed as wild Indians to raid the Settlers Stoll." Clarissa took a deep breath. "We share and swap, too. There will be something perfect for you."

Her head spinning from all the Brody's Crossing history,

Scarlett argued, "I'm not a resident. Won't people resent me intruding on their traditions? Some of them are already angry at me just for styling their hair a little differently."

"That's only a few people with more time than sense. Never mind them."

"I don't know…"

"She's got a point, Clarissa," Venetia said. "Some people don't like strangers coming in."

Clarissa dismissed Venetia with a wave. "The more the merrier for the Settlers Stroll, I say."

Scarlett shook her head as she walked toward the front of the salon. "The only 'settler' I could possibly consider being is one of those flashy saloon girls. I doubt there's a costume for that."

Maybe now Clarissa would stop asking her to get involved in Brody's Crossing holiday events.

JAMES HAD NO EXCUSE to see Scarlett on Thursday, since no other unhappy hair victims came into his office. However, his mother mentioned that her friends had seen him in a "compromising situation" with "that redheaded hairdresser" on Wednesday afternoon.

"I drove Scarlett around town and showed her some of the ranches," he told his mom.

"They said you two seemed very friendly with each other."

"Scarlett is my friend. That's all." He'd acted irresponsibly, leaving the office like that, but wasn't about to admit his temporary lapse of judgment. When he wasn't busy with a case or with a client, he thought about their kiss. She'd had such a stunned expression on her face when she'd left the car and hurried back to the salon.

"She's just here for a short time, and you've only known her a few days," his mother reminded him.

"I know. Don't worry, Mom."

Despite the fact that he was flirting with temptation, he had to follow up on the party invitation. Not that he wanted to retract his offer to take Scarlett to Dewey's. He wanted to be with her, socially or otherwise. He knew intimacy wasn't a wise choice for them; at the same time, he wasn't sure that knowledge would stop him from kissing her again.

On Friday he left a few minutes early for lunch so he could stop by the salon.

He paused just outside the window of Clarissa's House of Style. The brightly colored lights framed Scarlett, who wore a jaunty Santa hat with her green sweater and jeans. The little belly button ring twinkled in the overhead lights. As she brushed out the curls of Mrs. Casale, who owned the grocery store with her husband, James smiled at the picture Scarlett presented. She looked as out of place as the blue-and-yellow parakeet he'd seen at his mother's bird feeder did among a flock of sparrows. But Scarlett seemed perfectly at home, especially at Christmastime, with her red hair and green sweater and built-in sparkle.

"Hi," he said, after walking in.

Her smile faded and her eyes got round as she stopped brushing Mrs. Casale's hair. "Um, hi."

"Are you free for lunch?"

"No! Sorry, but I have someone else coming in soon."

"Then I guess I'll have to talk to you between customers again," he said, using his best smile. "Hello, Mrs. Casale."

"Good to see you, James." She looked at him above her bifocals. "Is that a new hairstyle you're sporting?"

"Why, yes it is. Scarlett cut my hair the other day." He ran his hands through the choppy strands. "Do you like it?"

"You look a little like Ty Pennington. He's a hottie."

"Good to know," James replied, his smile fading as he wondered what Mrs. Casale considered "hot."

"Is this about the Christmas party?" Scarlett asked.

"Yes. I need to see what time to pick you up."

"Well," she said, concentrating on fluffing her customer's hair, "about that. I told Clarissa that I'd go with her."

He felt his smile fade like ice cream on a hot day. "I thought we were going together."

She held up a comb. "I never agreed."

"Hmm, I must have misread your intentions." Would that be while she was so busy exploring his mouth?

"You might want to stand away," she said, brandishing a can of hair spray. He stepped back and she sprayed Mrs. Casale's dark blond hair.

He smiled at the grocery store owner as she gave Scarlett a tip, looked him over one more time, then went to pay Clarissa. He stepped closer as Scarlett swept clippings from the linoleum.

"Why don't you want to go with me?" he asked, moving near so they could have a semiprivate conversation.

"I just don't think it's a good idea."

"You thought spending time together was a good idea two days ago, when you asked me to drive you around."

"Yes, I did, but I guess it wasn't."

He leaned even closer and said softly in her ear, "Because of the kiss, right?"

She moved back with her broom and long-handled dustpan. "That wasn't a good idea, either."

He silently agreed with her, but didn't voice his opinion. "We had a good time. I didn't read any more into it than that," he assured her.

She took a deep breath, which made her short sweater rise an inch or so above her waistline. Enough for him to see the little silver moon and gold star in her belly button ring. Oh, boy. Was he in trouble. Despite what his lips were saying, his body wanted more than to drive around, chat and have a good time.

"Hey, my eyes are up here," she declared. He looked away from her tempting flesh into her angry eyes.

"I'm sorry. It's just…" He took a deep breath. "We don't see many of those around here."

"Waists?"

"No, those rings. Those little charms. In your belly button." He frowned. "Didn't that hurt?"

"Yes, but not for long. Now look, Mr. Curious. I'm sorry if I made you think I was looking for more than just some friendly time together."

"You didn't." He'd come up with ideas on his own.

"I really am leaving soon," she said softly, then caught her bottom lip between her teeth. Her bravado deflated. "It's just…I ran into a roadblock with Claude." Her eyes filled with tears and she blinked quickly. Then she sniffed delicately and turned away.

James put a hand on her shoulder. "What's wrong, sweetheart?"

She hugged her arms around her middle and hurried out of the salon area, to the room where she slept. James followed, unsure if she would stop or continue out the back door.

She halted and turned. Sniffed again. "He hasn't been able to find an engine." She lifted her big, luminous eyes to James. "If I have to buy a new car, it's going to take all the money I need to find an apartment and live on until I get my first paycheck, which won't be all that much, since I'm on an internship." She paused and sniffed yet again. "I don't think I can get my car fixed."

"Ah, sweetheart, please don't cry," he said softly, folding

her in his arms. She kept her own arms firmly around her middle, so it wasn't much of an embrace. More like a comforting hug. Poor Scarlett. Her big dreams were threatened and she was all alone.

She should have family around her, he thought fiercely. Family and friends who could help her emotionally and financially. "I know things seem bad right now, but we'll find a way. Even if it doesn't seem like it right now, there's more than one answer."

"I don't know how," she said, her voice muffled by his shirt and jacket. "I should have paid more attention to the gauges. It's my fault."

"No, it's not. The car is old, right? Technically, maybe you could have noticed the gauges a few minutes earlier, but you still would have been out on a fairly deserted road."

"Also my fault, for taking the wrong turn and deciding to drive all the way up to Oklahoma on a rural route."

"Those kinds of things happen. Hey, you weren't lost, were you? You knew where you were going and how to get there, didn't you? You were very resourceful, and instead of falling apart or calling someone to come rescue you, you got a job with Clarissa. You do your best to give everyone from teenagers to senior citizens an updated style so they'll feel better about themselves."

"I just fix hair. I'm not a social worker," she claimed, leaning back. She unwound her arms to wipe her eyes, which were a little smeared with some kind of eye makeup. He thought she looked adorable, which made him realize he *was* in way over his head.

When had Scarlett become adorable and compassionate and so…personal? Why couldn't he have stopped at quirky and lust-inducing? He'd lost once with a woman who didn't share his values and dreams. He wasn't about to risk anything—his time, his heart, or his reputation—on someone who was just passing through. He'd forgotten that the other day when he'd kissed her in broad daylight, when he'd laughed about the bridge-playing ladies seeing them together. He would remember it from now on.

Just because something made you feel good temporarily didn't mean it was good for you. Ice cream, chocolate chip cookies, alcohol and Scarlett included.

"Look, if you still want to go to Dewey's Christmas party with Clarissa, I understand. In the meantime, I'll check with Claude and see if we can think of alternatives."

Scarlett patted her eyes dry and looked up. "Okay. That would be great. Just don't *do* anything without my approval. I mean, with the car."

"No, of course not. I'm just trying to be a good friend. Friends try to help out, right?"

"Right." She frowned a little, then stepped back.

"I'll see you tomorrow night," he said.

"Okay."

"Well, I'd better get going. I'm off my lunch schedule," he said with a slight grin that probably fell flat. Who was he trying to convince that he was in a carefree mood—himself or Scarlett?

Chapter Five

On Saturday, Scarlett's one o'clock cut and style arrived accompanied by her hovering mother. Scarlett watched as the girl's father dropped them off at the door. He drove a Ford F150 pickup and looked as worried as his wife.

Bemused, Scarlett adjusted her reindeer antlers, softened the spikes in her hair and pulled her long-sleeved red T-shirt down past her waist. No sense alarming the folks even more. She didn't want the mother to swoon over a belly button ring. Or stare, as James had yesterday.

James. Darn him. He came on strong, telling her how she made him feel great, and kissing her in broad daylight, then backing away from going to the Christmas party with her as fast as his topsiders would carry him.

The frail looking girl, perhaps ten years old, stared at Scarlett with wide eyes as Clarissa smiled and pointed to a chair. The mother put a supporting arm around her as they tentatively approached.

"Hi! You must be my one o'clock appointment," Scarlett said cheerfully. "I'm Scarlett."

Both mother and daughter focused on her red hair.

"My name is Jennifer Wright. This is my daughter, Hailey." The woman carefully removed a fleecy hat from

Hailey's head. "Her hair is growing back in and it's gotten long enough to need a little trim."

Scarlett stifled a gasp. The girl's thin, blond hair was obviously growing back from chemotherapy. No wonder she seemed so pale and frail. Oh, poor baby. Scarlett wanted to hug the girl and tell her everything would be okay.

Which was so obviously the wrong thing to do. "Oh, it is! What a pretty color, too."

"I like the color of *your* hair," Hailey said in a surprisingly strong voice. "I love the color red, and your style is just so…phat!"

Scarlett chuckled at the compliment. "If I had pretty blond hair like yours, I'd just keep it that way forever." That was almost true. She'd tried light blond, but her coloring wasn't right. She'd looked like an albino Italian pixie with her light olive skin and short curls.

"Mommy, can I have red hair? My old hair was kind of reddish-blond, wasn't it?"

"Well, yes, a very light strawberry-blond."

"My hair grew back different. Can it be red again?"

"You can't have red hair, Hailey. It would look odd— on you, I mean. It's fine for Miss Scarlett."

Scarlett laughed. "Please, just Scarlett. Otherwise, I feel as if I stepped off the set of *Gone With the Wind*. I'm from Atlanta, you know?"

She hunkered down so she was eye level with Hailey. "You know, your new hair is still growing in and I know it's different. But you know what? Lots of girls and women pay a lot of money for pretty, soft blond hair like yours. I think that we should let it grow back a little more, see what it looks like by summer. If we tried to make it red right now, it would probably break and get all dull and wouldn't be as pretty as it is now."

"Can you fix it so it doesn't just flop all over my head?"

"I sure can. I'll cut it and show you how to use a gentle product to get it to behave just like you want."

"Okay then. It doesn't have to be red like yours."

Scarlett looked up at Jennifer and saw her breathe a sigh of relief. The two of them shared a smile.

"Come on up here in my chair," Scarlett said to Hailey. "Let's take a look at your brand-new hair. How exciting, to get new hair!"

As she swirled a cape around Hailey's thin shoulders, she noticed Venetia across the aisle, blinking back a tear.

THE CROWD AT DEWEY'S WAS in full celebration mode when James pushed his way through the door at eight o'clock Saturday night. His "date" pressed close to his back. "I'm moving as fast as I can," he told her.

"It's cold out here, James," his mother complained.

Finally, he managed to close the massive, rough wood door behind them. His mother shuddered. She never could stand the cold, but wouldn't wear the down-insulated, all-weather coat he'd gotten her last year. "I look like a sausage," she'd told him, and gone back to her tried-and-true wool coat, thin leather gloves and plaid scarf.

At least he wasn't that much of a slave to tradition. Tonight, for example, he'd purposefully worn a bright red plaid Western shirt with mother-of-pearl snaps, and new Levi's. Entirely different than the button-down-collar shirts and the chinos he normally wore to the office. Plus, he'd finger-combed and shaped his hair, duplicating the style that Scarlett had intended, even exaggerating the choppy tufts a little more than she'd done.

"Oh, look," his mother said. "There's Ida Bell and Venetia at a table. Let's join them."

James escorted his mother through the happy crowd, getting some back slaps and "hellos" on the way. Apparently the Dewey's crowd had come considerably earlier than the eight o'clock advertised time to get in prime party mode.

He greeted several friends and clients on the way to Ida and Venetia's table. Beside them, Troy Crawford stood with his arm around his fiancée, Raven York. James had recently learned they'd planned a "destination wedding" someplace tropical next May. Troy had said something about swimming with rescued dolphins. It sounded like fun, since they didn't have much family except Troy's brother, Cal, who was in the military. Troy said Raven's mother was flying down from New Hampshire for the ceremony with several of Raven's friends.

James knew that if he were to ever remarry, he'd plan something right here in Brody's Crossing so all his family, friends and neighbors could attend. Not that he had any plans to tie to knot. First he'd have to find a sweet, attractive and understanding woman who wanted to stay right here. No more climbing the professional or social ladder. When he and Babs had married, her family in Fort Worth had insisted on a large church wedding for three hundred of their closest friends.

At least the bride's family had paid for that extravaganza. He didn't have anything against his former in-laws, so he hoped his former father-in-law had at least paid off the wedding before the divorce was finalized.

"Merry Christmas, everyone," he said once his mother had greeted their friends.

"Good to see you," Troy said, shaking his hand. James could see him checking out his hair, but he didn't say anything.

"I thought you might have a date," Ida added.

"No, just my mom. Dad's hip is acting up with all this cold weather."

"Hmm," Venetia said, loudly enough to be heard over the music. "You sure did try to talk *someone* into a date."

All eyes turned to him for confirmation, but he just shrugged. "Let me buy a round of drinks," he offered to change the subject.

As he looked for a waitress who could bring them cocktails, soft drinks or beer, he knew he had to talk to Scarlett sooner or later. He had some information he needed to share.

He heard the people at the table talking, heard chairs scraping on the hardwood floor, and tried to scan the smoky room for someone who could bring him a much-needed drink.

Twila came by and everyone ordered, then James found a chair and pulled it up next to Raven. "How are you enjoying your first Texas Christmas?" he asked.

"It's very…lively," she answered, pushing her long black hair behind her shoulder.

Troy leaned forward. "What she means is she can't wait to get back to her quiet farm and attend a modest gathering at a quaint New Hampshire inn."

James laughed, then let his eyes wander again. Who was he looking for this time? He was afraid he knew the answer to that one: another stranger in town. Another person who'd come west and was stuck here, at least for a while. She probably wouldn't be around for Christmas, though, and that shouldn't bother him as much as it did.

"Why, look who's here!" Ida exclaimed. "Clarissa, come join us!" She waved her arm. "Oh, it looks as if that new hairdresser is with her."

"Have you met her?" James's mother asked.

"No. She sure is different."

"Different can be good," Raven said, glancing at Troy.

James stood up and turned toward where Ida was waving. He took in Scarlett's appearance with a hungry gaze and gut-clenching reaction. She wore a form-fitting, long-sleeved, white velvet top with a fake-fur neckline. Her dark, tight jeans hit just below her waistline. The little silver moon and gold star belly button ring twinkled in the Christmas lights strung along Dewey's rough-hewn rafters. Her red hair sparkled, even in the dimly lit bar.

He thought he'd be okay with seeing her again, now that he'd convinced himself there could be nothing more than casual friendship between them.

He'd been wrong.

SCARLETT STOPPED NEXT TO the crowded table where James's friends sat with beers, cocktails and soft drinks. Ida motioned for one of the guys to pull up a couple more chairs, which was getting difficult because of the crowd. Apparently the whole town turned out for the annual Christmas shindig.

Clarissa tugged over a chair and squeezed in between Venetia and Ida. That left Scarlett to sit by James and a very pretty woman with a pale complexion and long black hair. His date? But no, when she leaned toward the man beyond and smiled, Scarlett felt herself relax.

This was not a good reaction. She shouldn't care if James had a date, since Scarlett had turned down his invitation.

With a sigh, she took her seat.

"Everyone," Clarissa said in a loud voice, "in case you haven't met her, this is Scarlett. She's working at the salon for a while."

"Scarlett, do you know Troy Crawford and Raven York?" James asked.

"Pleased to meet you," she murmured.

Introductions went around. People talked about the crowd, the cold weather, and the chances that the tinsel-clad peppermint sticks on the posts downtown would hold up for one more Christmas season. Scarlett ordered a Diet Coke, and everyone asked her if she'd be their designated driver. She laughed and told them that the last car she'd driven had ended up in Claude McCaskie's garage.

"That reminds me," James said. "I have some information about your car situation. Would you be interested in finding a quiet place to discuss it?"

"Uh, sure." She wasn't at all certain that she wanted to get up and leave with James, but she needed to know what he'd found out.

"Folks, I'm going to update Scarlett on her car options I just found out about," he told the table in general.

"Sure, if that's what they're calling it now, go right ahead," Venetia said with a chuckle.

"Seriously, it's about her car," James claimed.

"Don't get all defensive. I'm just teasing," the other stylist said.

"It should be quiet in the back, by the pool tables," he said, touching Scarlett's elbow as they got up. He leaned close and said in her ear, "There are no speakers there, and almost everyone is out here, socializing."

She didn't care what words he said; shivers went down her spine when she felt his breath on her neck and ear.

They made their way to the rear of Dewey's, James receiving greetings from people she assumed were friends and clients. He had a lot of them. She remembered how he felt about this town, and wasn't surprised that he knew so many folks. A couple of them even commented on his hair, which made her feel good.

He found a niche between the emergency exit and the pool cue rack. As James had predicted, few people were playing billiards. Almost everyone was in the Christmas spirit. "You have news?" she asked, leaning against the wall.

"Claude found an engine from a junkyard just south of Dallas. The car was rear-ended a couple of years ago, so it's not in the most pristine condition. According to the former owner, though, it worked great before the wreck."

"Won't that be a lot of work, to get it into my car and make it run again?"

"It could be. It's one of those things—you never know how well it works until you try. These used parts don't come with guarantees. However, Claude seems to think that he can make it work."

"Should I put my faith in Claude?"

"I can't make that decision for you," James said earnestly. "I can only tell you that he is a good mechanic."

Scarlett let out a sigh of frustration and looked away. "What are my other options?"

"Claude also looked at the car auction for a good used vehicle that might have some damage. He found two that he thought would be good for you. He thinks both of them would get you to California safely."

"These have been wrecked?"

"One was hit in the side, the other needs an overhaul and some parts. Both would be about the same price as the engine for the Mercedes."

"I don't know. I never learned much about cars. My dad…well, he always made those decisions. For all of us. My brother and sister don't know anything about cars, either, not to mention my mother."

Her dad was such a traditionalist that he believed the man of the house needed to have all the knowledge about auto and household repairs, tools and maintenance. And if he did his job of raising children right, they'd be so successful they wouldn't need to know about such things. That might be okay for the doctor and the accountant, but not the lowly hairdresser, who couldn't afford to hire people to do everyday chores.

Her dad wasn't mean about it; he just automatically took care of everyone. Scarlett thought he was too much of a control freak. Why couldn't he have asked if his children were interested in cars and lawns and tools?

Not that she *was* interested, but still…

"I'm no expert, but I'll be glad to go with you to see Claude on Monday. Or hey, maybe you'd like to call and talk to your father. He might have an idea—"

"No! I mean…well, I don't want to tell him the Benz is on the blink. He picked out that car for my high school graduation present. It was used, but in great condition. He wanted something big and safe. He took it to get oil changes regularly and checked the tire pressure weekly. I'm telling you, he loved that car."

"Maybe he just loved the idea that you had a safe car."

Scarlett looked away, studying the design on the worn, green-and-brown carpet. "Maybe. But whatever, I don't want to tell him that I let the engine die a quick and painful death in Texas."

"Whatever you feel comfortable with. I'm just here to help if you want me to." She looked back up in time to see James smile. "Or give you a ride when you're bored."

She forced herself to smile in return. "You're a good friend. Let me think about the car situation over the weekend. I'll go see Claude Monday morning."

"Okay." James stood there in front of her, and the moment grew awkward. She felt as if she should say something else, but what? He was being friendly. Nothing more. So why did she feel as if she wanted to grab that red plaid shirt and kiss him senseless? As she stared at it, she realized the shirt had pearlized snaps, not buttons. Snaps. Oh, that was very dangerous.

"We'd better get back to the party," she said, before she did something stupid. "You were right—this is one event I wouldn't want to miss."

"No, of course not," he said softly, still looking at her. He shoved his hands in his pockets and stepped back. "Come on. Maybe I'll talk you into dancing later."

"Maybe." But she knew she wouldn't dance with James tonight. Too risky. She'd find some good-natured cowboy she didn't care about, and they'd dance and laugh. She'd be polite with James, but careful. He'd made himself clear about his priorities, and she had her own goals.

Goals that didn't include sticking around a small Texas town when she had a chance to make it as the next stylist to the stars in exciting L.A.

SCARLETT HAD A NICE DAY off on Sunday, sleeping in, having breakfast at the café and then taking herself to a family-friendly movie at the old-fashioned Rialto Theater. She saw a fairly good comedy, ate red hots and drank a big Diet Coke. Most of the other theatergoers were couples with one or more children, although there were some teens. The atmosphere was so small-town, so idyllic. She wondered if she looked as out of place as she felt.

The weather was nice, so after the movie she stopped by the little park next to James's office and sat on a bench. This time of year, there wasn't much foliage or any flowers except for some pansies in pots around the fountain. Several cedar trees were decorated with thin strings of popcorn and cranberries, and birds chirped and hopped among the branches.

The scene was very peaceful, albeit lonely, but soon she felt as if someone was watching her. The windows to James's office were dark, so he probably wasn't working. She looked around, then up. Had one of the blinds moved upstairs? She wasn't sure, but didn't like the idea of strangers watching her. Suddenly, she felt very alone. Downtown Brody's Crossing was nearly deserted on Sunday afternoon, and probably as safe as anywhere on earth. But still… She pushed herself up from the bench and reluctantly left the birds behind. She had some laundry to do, anyway.

A couple of minutes later, she unlocked the back door of the salon and discovered chaos. Clarissa and Venetia had multiple old-fashioned dresses hanging from the door frames and from hooks around the room. Bonnets were piled on the counter by the coffeemaker. Shoes and boots littered the floor.

"Oh, good. You're back!" her employer said, hurrying forward and grasping Scarlett's hands. "We need you to pick out your dress."

"Dress?"

"For the Settlers Stroll this evening. Don't tell me you forgot!"

Actually, she had. "I thought I mentioned that this wasn't a good idea."

"We'll have a great time," Clarissa insisted, forging ahead.

"You might as well give in," Venetia said with one of her throaty chuckles. "Clarissa's not giving up until you're laced in."

That sounded uncomfortable. "But—"

"Come on." Clarissa grabbed Scarlett's arm. "I have just the thing to make you shine."

AN HOUR LATER, the sun was setting and Scarlett was indeed laced into one of the most outrageous outfits she'd ever worn. Yards of red and purple satin, taffeta and net formed a skirt that flowed from a very fitted waist to the tops of lace-up boots. The purple bodice, equally fitted, had a round neckline accented by red sequins.

"How's the hat?" she asked, bending to see the whole concoction in the mirror.

"Pretty wild," Venetia said, checking out the arrangement of purple plumes, lace and red satin perched on Scarlett's head. She'd combed her hair back from her forehead and tucked it behind her ears so it wouldn't compete with the crazy hat, which was suitable for a circa 1900 Las Vegas showgirl act, if such a thing had ever existed.

"We've never had such a convincing showgirl," Clarissa said, walking back into the room with her shawl draped around her. "You look fabulous, as if you stepped out of the Dry Gulch Saloon."

"They'll probably run me out of town," Scarlett murmured, thinking of the families she'd seen at the theater. Not one potential saloon girl among them.

"You have a warped view of this town," Clarissa said, draping a heavy shawl around Scarlett's shoulders. "They're much more tolerant than you think."

Scarlett wasn't sure about that. In her experience, people were threatened by anything different. But she'd just bluff her way through the situation, if necessary.

"So, what do we do? Stroll around?" she asked.

"We're meeting just across the side street in front of the hardware store," Clarissa answered, pointing out the back door with her closed fan. "Then we're all strolling down Main Street to Memorial Park, then over to the community center for refreshments. Some of the businesses along the way will serve finger food and drinks."

Ordinarily, Scarlett would roll her eyes at this old-fashioned custom. She wasn't a period-costume kind of girl. But somehow, dressing up in the saloon gown, boots and hat was kind of funky.

"Okay, let's go," she said, hoping Clarissa didn't regret hauling her along for the stroll.

Venetia led the way. Clarissa, who looked like a friendly farmer's wife from the late nineteenth century, hooked her arm through Scarlett's. She leaned close and said, "Venetia told me what happened with Hailey."

"I hope you didn't get any complaints about her hair." James hadn't shown up to give her a lecture or a warning.

"No! I just wanted to say that you handled that so well, so sweet."

"Um, thanks." Scarlett didn't know what to say.

"Look who's here," Venetia said as they stepped beneath the canopy of the farmer's market. Old-fashioned metal lamps hung from long hooks over the windows, casting a warm glow over the assembled group.

Scarlett looked around, her gaze drawn to one tall figure in a turn-of-the-century dark suit, hat and cravat-style tie. The standing, pointed collar of his white shirt appeared to be poking a hole in his jaw as he looked down to talk to a shorter man.

James Brody looked good enough to make even a jaded saloon girl swoon. Scarlett slipped away from Clarissa, threw back her shoulders and sauntered up to the lawyer.

"Hey, mister," she said in a throaty voice. "Buy a girl a drink?"

Chapter Six

James couldn't have been more shocked if a real saloon girl had time-traveled to Brody's Crossing and materialized beside him. "Scarlett?"

"Who else would be crazy enough to wear this outfit?" she asked, chuckling.

"I don't know about crazy," he answered, "but definitely unique." She appeared as a bright, bright rose in a field of pastel flowers.

"Why, thank you, kind sir. That's the nicest thing you could say."

He didn't agree. Being different wasn't a real goal of his. But Scarlett had apparently decided to be outrageous tonight, and he wasn't going to chide her for it. "Scarlett, this is Mr. George Russell, president of the First National Bank of Brody's Crossing."

James speculated that George had never seen a saloon girl before, based on the banker's wide eyes. Or perhaps he was surprised that a conservative lawyer was friendly with a vivacious, colorful person such as Scarlett.

She held out her hand to the stunned-looking banker. "Nice to meet you, Mr. Russell."

"Er, good meeting you, Miss Scarlett."

As soon as they shook hands, the mayor, Toni Casale, announced the start of the procession. People would walk two abreast down the sidewalk to the park. She looked very dapper in what James had been told was a lady's walking dress.

"I'd better find the missus," the banker muttered, giving Scarlett another wide-eyed glance.

James looked at her. "I guess that leaves us."

"Um, you're not with anyone?"

"Why do you ask me that?"

"I don't know. Maybe because you're single and… everything."

He wasn't sure what "everything" entailed. "If you don't want to walk with me, just say so."

"No, I do." Scarlett shrugged. "I just thought—"

"Then let's go." He assumed she was about to make some unnecessary remark about how different they were.

He offered his arm, and after a startled glance, she tucked her hand inside his elbow.

James had seen Scarlett at the little park earlier in the day. She'd looked so alone sitting there, her bright red hair glistening in the winter sunlight, her hands clasped in her lap as she sat on the park bench. He'd stood in his kitchen, which faced west and overlooked the park, and wondered if he'd ever mentioned that he lived over the law office. He'd been about to go downstairs and talk to her when she'd jumped up and walked away.

Perhaps it was just as well that he hadn't spoken with her earlier. He would have invited her upstairs, and she might have actually accepted! And then what? Being in public with Scarlett was tempting enough, but being alone was dangerous to his peace of mind.

His mother had also hinted that "seeing" Scarlett could hurt his reputation. He wasn't sure about that. She was a stylist, not a criminal. Granted, she was different from other women he'd dated, but that wasn't exactly scandalous.

Not that he could keep people from talking…. However, not everyone in town loved to gossip. Only about half of the people on the Settlers Stroll tonight, he thought with a smile, would be talking about the saloon girl tomorrow.

"What's so funny?" Scarlett asked.

"Oh, nothing. Just enjoying our walk."

He noticed lots of friends. Raven, dressed as an Indian princess, walked arm in arm with Troy, who hadn't dressed up per se, but just donned cowboy apparel. Mr. and Mrs. McCall appeared stately and conservative in their "rich settlers" clothing. James recalled the look on their faces when a group of "wild Indians," as the townsfolk called them, had swooped down Main Street about twenty years ago.

Most people still didn't know who, besides Wyatt, had participated in that raid. James smiled and nodded at the McCalls, remembering the fun of running wild in the street. Of course, the loincloth had been a bit chilly….

Everyone stopped at city hall for store-bought cookies and pink punch, which was a little too sweet for his taste. Then most of the group split off to go to the hardware store, where Leo Casale, the mayor's brother, reportedly had assorted imported chocolates.

"Chocolates or hot chocolate?" James asked Scarlett.

"Hmm. Hard decision. Since I'm a little cool, I'll opt for the hot chocolate."

"Good choice." He steered her across Commerce Street, past the closed café. When he opened the door to a storefront, she paused.

"Hey, this is your office." She narrowed her eyes. "Hot chocolate isn't your code word for 'see my etchings,' is it?"

James laughed. "Absolutely not. Come in, and you'll

see. Besides, we're well chaperoned," he said, nodding to the group behind them.

His mother waited inside, an urn of hot chocolate, stacks of disposable cups and Christmas napkins ready. She'd also made and decorated sugar cookies. "Hi, Mom."

"Hello, Mrs. Brody," Scarlett said. "This looks really great."

"Thank you, Scarlett. James mentioned that you like hot chocolate," she said, with a meaningful glance in his direction.

His mother sometimes administered a few good jabs, but tonight he wasn't going to take the bait.

"The office looks nice," he said. She had decorated the reception area with a small Christmas tree, plus a Santa and a reindeer he remembered from his childhood. The little table was covered in fake snow.

"Thanks for taking care of this while I was at the farmers' market," he added. His mother hadn't wanted to get dressed up in a costume, anyway, but James enjoyed the tradition.

"You're welcome. I think we have some visitors."

They drank hot chocolate and ate several cookies, which were much better than the store-bought ones at the city hall. Before long, it was time to meet with everyone else at the park.

The wind had picked up while they were inside, and Scarlett moved closer, feeling chilly with just a shawl over her sleeveless dress. She didn't know what to expect, especially when a man James identified as the minister of the community church stepped up on the concrete planter box at the end of the park.

"Thank you for coming to the annual Settlers Stroll. This is the time during the evening when we reflect on the past and give thanks for what we have today."

As Scarlett listened to the man talk about the founders and their hardships, she thought about her own situation. She'd been traveling west like so many people over a hundred years ago. She'd broken down, like a horse that had gone lame or a wagon that had lost a wheel. Unlike the settlers, she had a profession, so she could work. Also unlike them, she had a fairly comfortable place to stay, people to help her, and other ways to get where she was going.

She had a lot to be thankful for, she realized as the minister ended his short talk with a prayer. She barely noticed when James enclosed her fingers in his warm ones, but as she raised her head after the "amen," she realized they were standing very near and actually holding hands in public.

"I saw you in the park earlier in the day," he said.

"That was you I felt watching me?"

"You noticed?" One eyebrow quirked up and then he nodded. "I wasn't spying."

"I believe you," she said softly, leaning closer. She'd felt lonely after the movie, seeing the families. Now she was surrounded by people, and the only person she wanted to be with was right beside her.

And she didn't need to encourage him. For some reason—maybe the one that said "opposites attract"—she tempted him. Maybe he only desired her in a physical sense. She wasn't sure what he wanted, and maybe she didn't know what she wanted with him, either.

Santa, all I want for Christmas is a hunky lawyer. She should wish for something more practical, like a new engine.

"Time to go!" Clarissa said, bustling through the crowd. "Time to get to the community center."

When everyone started filing out of the little park toward the community center, Scarlett lagged behind. "Maybe I should go on back to the salon."

"No! Why don't you want to join us?" James asked in surprise.

"Because I'm not one of you, despite the costume."

He looked at her in the darkness, and suddenly she felt silly. All those insecurities. All the doubts about acceptance... About him. "Oh, okay. I'll go the community center with you. Just don't try any funny stuff," she warned with mock severity.

"Scarlett, please—" he began, but she cut him off.

"I told you I'd go. Let's get over there before everything is gone." She grabbed his hand and pulled. "Although I'm not sure I can eat anything after those yummy cookies your mother made."

James looked as though he wanted to say something else, but thankfully, he didn't.

She hurried after the cheerful folks strolling down the street.

"DID YOU HEAR what Venetia said?" his mother asked later at the community center, while Scarlett was in the ladies room.

"No, I didn't."

"She was telling us about little Hailey Wright. That's Jennifer Hopkins's—well, now Jennifer Wright's—daughter."

"What about her?" He saw Jennifer around town every now and then. He didn't remember seeing her daughter lately.

Venetia returned with a cup of green, frothy punch. "She came into the salon yesterday to get her first haircut and style after her chemo treatments."

"No, I hadn't realized she was back home. Is she okay?"

"She's still weak, but getting better," Venetia said. "The thing is, you'd think a wild child like Scarlett wouldn't be good with a frail little girl like that, but it was the darnedest thing. Hailey took to her right away, and Scarlett was just as gentle as could be. Wouldn't let the little girl get her hair

dyed red, styled into spikes or anything weird. She compli-
mented Hailey until she was grinning from ear to ear."

"Scarlett's really very nice," James said.

Venetia shook her head. "I've sure changed my mind. I
didn't think she was all that great for business, or good to
have around, but now I do."

"Well, maybe we won't have as many people coming
into the office, complaining about their hair," James's
mother said.

"Oh, I wouldn't hold your breath. Some people just
love to complain," he replied, thinking of those who were
still a bit lawsuit-crazy. With any luck, there would be no
more talk about a class action suit. And with more stories
like the one Venetia had told, soon Scarlett would be seen
as someone other than a wild, red-haired stranger.

Scarlett returned to the small group, followed by Clarissa.
Within moments James excused himself. He wanted to talk
to other men for a while. He needed a break from Scarlett's
flashy saloon girl costume, which made her all too tempting.

But on the other hand, he knew her vulnerability, shown
in her forced good humor and full-speed-ahead attitude,
was even more compelling. If he wasn't careful, he'd start
caring way too much about someone who would be out of
his life in a flash.

So he'd talk to Rodney Bell and Troy Crawford for a
while, then escort Scarlett back to the salon, unless she
walked with Clarissa and Venetia. He wouldn't get in
trouble with Scarlett, his mother or her friends if he remembered to behave himself.

JAMES STAYED AWAY as long as he could on Monday, but
since he had to get out, anyway, he walked to the salon to
see if Scarlett was selling or keeping the Mercedes. He

didn't like the feeling that his curiosity could get the best of him. But he didn't seem to possess his usual self-control around a certain redhead.

He walked up the steps to the little back porch so he wouldn't draw too much attention to himself and Scarlett by standing in front of the big picture window for everyone to see. He was just about to knock on the door when it burst open, nearly toppling him backward. He instinctively reached out and grasped the woman bolting toward him: Scarlett.

"Hey, what's up?" he asked as she gasped. He quickly released her upper arms as they both steadied themselves.

"I…I just needed to get away for a while," she said almost breathlessly. Was there a thread of desperation in her voice?

"What's wrong?"

"It's Venetia and Clarissa," she said, hugging her arms around herself. "They're just being so darned *nice*."

James frowned, but said, "I can see how that would be irritating."

She huffed out a breath, jammed her fists in the pocket of her hoodie and marched past him. Descending the stairs, she muttered, "It's no big deal."

He followed her. "It sounds like a big deal."

She whirled to face him. "Not that I'm irritated, but what they're being nice about. I just did Hailey's hair, okay? I've done chemo patients before, so I just happened to know what to do."

"Still, Clarissa and Venetia appreciated the way you handled it."

"It's no big deal, except maybe to Hailey."

He reached for Scarlett's arm to slow her. "Don't you think it's a compliment? They admire you. They said so last night at the community center."

"What?" She appeared even more confused and outraged.

Maybe he shouldn't have admitted that Venetia had talked about her, but really, he'd thought Scarlett would be flattered. "She just mentioned Hailey's hair appointment."

"Oh, I just hate being talked about like that. Like I'm a child or a freak or something."

"No one thinks you're a child or a freak."

"They all think I'm weird."

"Original—that's how they saw you. You're from out of town, you're colorful and gregarious and kind." He grinned, hoping she'd take the final remark in good spirits. "Your red hair alone is certain to give you celebrity status."

"I don't want to *be* a celebrity. I just want to do their hair."

"Things are different in a small town."

Scarlett took a deep breath, exhaled…and seemed to relax. "You're right. If I wanted to blend in, I'd have mousey-brown hair and neutral clothes."

"And no belly button ring," he added before thinking.

"What?"

"Never mind." He took her arm again and started steering her toward the parking spaces behind his office. "So you don't have any clients for a while?"

"No, not until after school."

"Then come along. We'll grab some lunch and you can visit a client with me. I have a one o'clock appointment at a ranch near Graham. I think my client would love to meet you."

"I don't know…"

"Come on. You don't have anything better to do, and you can fill me in on what's going on with your car."

"Oh, okay. But I'm not sure I want to visit with your client. I mean, is that legal?"

James laughed. "Let me worry about legalities."

"I CAN'T BELIEVE HOW GOOD this tastes," Scarlett said after swallowing another bite of her taquito. The chicken filling was moist and the outside was crispy. After dunking it in some of the best salsa she'd ever tasted, she could just swoon.

"Have you tried the tamales?"

"Not yet."

"I know we're in a bit of a hurry, but don't miss them."

"Yum, I won't. After days of cookies, burgers and breakfast food, this tastes so good."

James had suggested the little Mexican restaurant on the highway to Graham as a quick place to get a bite to eat. The client he was seeing at one o'clock was just a few miles away.

"Are you sure I can't just sit here and eat while you have your appointment?"

"No. You'd eat too much, get sick and throw up in my SUV on the way back to Brody's Crossing."

"No, I wouldn't," she said, licking her fingertips. "You sound like my father."

"That's a nice thing to tell a guy."

"Oh, come on. You know what I mean."

James gave her a narrow-eyed look, but didn't say anything else "preachy."

"I'm going to have Claude get that engine from Dallas and repair my car," she said, after finishing her taquito and reaching for a tamale.

"Okay. I'm sure he'll do a good job."

"It's going to take awhile."

"Working on older cars usually does. I remember the Pontiac I had in college. That thing was put together with baling wire and bubble gum. Whenever I needed a part for it, the mechanic I used had to find some way to make something fit. I'm no good at car repair, so I had to depend on him."

"Same here, except my father is the one who dealt with

the family cars. He knew all the local mechanics. I was glad to let him take care of everything. Now I wish I knew a little more, especially since I'm really far from home."

"As I said, Claude is trustworthy. He's been in business forever."

Scarlett knew people who had been in business forever who weren't all that good at doing their jobs, but they were more artistic than functional, so she guessed that didn't compare with Claude's particular talent. Why did everyone think that longer was better? What was wrong with trying something new? But she was projecting her own issues again, so she told herself to stop thinking and keep enjoying the delicious food before James made her go on his appointment with his client.

"Tell me more about becoming a judge."

"I'm not becoming a judge, I'm just sitting in for one. Judge Bell asked me to take his bench while he's on vacation—a special Christmas trip with his grandchildren."

"When is this going to happen?" she asked.

"The week of December 17." James motioned to the waiter for the check.

"Next week?"

"That's right. I probably won't have much to do, but the court is going to be open that week. There's a case that may need some rulings for an upcoming trial in January. They want to make sure nothing holds up the proceedings."

"I hope Claude can get my car fixed next week," she said as she dug around in her purse for her wallet.

"When will your new engine get here?"

"Claude has to go fetch it. I think he's going tomorrow afternoon." She grabbed a ten and placed it on the table.

"No way," James said. "This was my treat."

"I want to pay for my lunch."

"I invited you. I pay."

"This isn't a date."

"No, but we're friends. I was going to lunch anyway. I appreciate the company."

"I want—"

"Put that on your car repair bill," James insisted. "I think you'll need it."

Scarlett slumped in the seat. "You're right. It's going to be a doozy." She wouldn't have to spend all of her savings to pay for the repairs, but she wouldn't have much to get started in L.A., either. She'd find a way, though. She always did.

Paying off her student loan for cosmetology school had taken her months. She'd moved back home, eaten few meals out and hadn't socialized much during that time. Now she was debt free, which was better than some of her friends, who used their credit cards for everything. She'd saved her money so she'd have options when something good came up, which she'd always known would happen.

And now something good was waiting for her in California, if only she could get there.

She must have been deep in thought, because when she looked up, James had already paid the check and placed several bills on the table. "Ready?" he asked.

"If you insist."

"I do. I won't be responsible for overdosing on Maria's chipotle salsa."

"Okay." Scarlett groaned in grand theatrical style as she scooted out of the bench seat. James chuckled, and her spirits lifted.

The drive to the small, run-down ranch didn't take long. Scarlett took it all in—the sagging fences, the overgrown weeds, the siding in need of a coat of paint. Still, she could tell that at one time in the near past, this house and the ranch surrounding it had been well-kept.

James put the SUV in Park and turned off the engine. "Wade and Phyllis Holmes are both my clients. I did their wills last year, but since then, a problem has come up. Wade has some medical issues and the doctors have had trouble getting his meds regulated. If he seems... confused, don't worry, and don't make a big deal out of it."

"Okay."

"Mrs. Holmes—Phyllis—is really nice. I'm sure you'll like her."

"Good. But I still don't see why you wanted me to come out here with you."

"Just come on. If they don't mind you listening to us discuss their case, then legally, there's no problem. Besides, I think they'll like you."

Scarlett opened her door and jumped down before James could come around and act all gentlemanly. Okay, it wasn't an act—he *was* a gentleman.

They walked together to the door and James knocked. In just a moment, it was opened by a petite, short-haired woman who appeared to be in her mid-sixties. She wore a purple tunic sweater, leggings and gold tennis shoes. "James Brody!" she exclaimed, reaching for him. She pulled him inside the doorway, then turned to Scarlett with a big smile. "And who did you bring to visit?"

"This is Scarlett No-last-name from Atlanta. She's a hair-stylist and a friend of mine. I hope you don't mind. Her car is being repaired and she wanted to go to lunch with me."

"I—" she started to say, but Phyllis cut her off.

"Really? Well, isn't that interesting? Call me Phyllis. Come on in."

"I didn't bring her here to do your hair, so don't pressure her," James warned with good-natured teasing.

"Oh, darn. Well, I don't have much hair to begin with. Come on into the sunroom and see Wade. He just had his lunch and he's watching his soaps."

Phyllis bustled ahead of Scarlett and James, picking up newspapers, shooing a tiger-striped cat off the sofa in the living room they passed through. "Wade, we've got company," she said in a loud voice. "James Brody and his friend are here. I'm going to get them some tea."

"No, that's okay," Scarlett tried to say, but Phyllis was already gone.

They stepped down into the sunroom, which had been converted from a porch, it seemed. Wade Holmes sat in a recliner, a TV tray next to the wide arm. An older model tube television sat across the room, next to a big, unruly plant. Sunlight streamed in the aluminum-frame windows.

Phyllis bustled back with four glasses of iced tea, which she set on the TV tray. "Here, let's turn that television off." She commandeered the remote and switched off the flickering signal.

"But my show!" Wade said, reaching out.

"Sweetie, you know you can catch up in the next few weeks. The plots move so slow, you can figure out who's done what to who without any problem."

"Hi, James."

"Hello, Wade. How are you today?"

"Having a good day, except for my bossy wife."

Phyllis smiled and swatted him on the shoulder. "You sweet-talkin' devil, you." She turned to Scarlett. "He's cranky when I mess with his soaps."

"I can see that." She looked down at Wade, then took a seat in a nearby straight-back chair. "Are you sure it's okay if I'm here? I can wait outside."

"No, we don't have any secrets from James or a friend of his."

James sat on the sofa near Wade and leaned forward. "I have some options to discuss with you about your property," he said. "We can take action now to keep your nephew from going any further."

"Sounds good," Wade said. "Money hungry little bas—"

"Now, Wade, don't start cussin' a blue streak," Phyllis warned her husband. Again she turned to Scarlett. "Although I have to admit, there's no love lost between any of us about this. Did James tell you what that little skunk is tryin' to do?"

"Er, no, not really."

"He wants this ranch. He thinks he can get it by saying that Wade isn't capable of running it anymore. Well, he can't have it! It's ours."

"That's right, and we're going to see that it stays that way," James said. "Now, first we need to get the property to a manageable size, as we discussed before. Then, we need to get you some income. I have some ideas for both."

"Oh, good. We're ready to fight."

"That's what I want to hear," James said with a smile.

Chapter Seven

"That's a really nice thing you're doing for the Holmeses," Scarlett said as James pulled out onto the highway to drive back to town.

"They're clients. This is not a pro bono case."

"Yes, but Phyllis told me in the kitchen that you're not charging them much at all, and you've done all kinds of work."

He shrugged. "Some cases are more difficult than others. This one required some creative thinking."

"You, a financial planner, a gas and oil leasing agent, a real estate broker, a banker and who else?"

"Oh, just that new remodeling contractor from Graham."

"The house is going to look great," she said, thinking about the plans James and the Holmeses had discussed for their home. When they finished with the mineral leases, the sale of part of the property, the updates and the reverse mortgage, Wade and Phyllis would have enough money to live on and provide care for him. And best of all, by the time they were old and gone from this earth, their estate would be reduced to near nothing and their slimy nephew wouldn't get enough inheritance to fill his money-grubbing fist.

Poetic justice, Scarlett thought. She'd liked the Holmeses,

and they'd liked her. Best of all, she'd learned that although Phyllis had moved to the area after marrying Wade in her hometown of Phoenix, she felt part of the community. She and Wade wanted to live here forever, and with James's help, they would.

Oh, James. What was she going to do about her growing feelings for him? Scarlett wondered. He was just so darn nice. She wanted to say that he was too preppy, too conservative, too boring for her. When she was with him, though, she kept seeing all of his good qualities. He was intelligent, kind and thoughtful to everyone. He was a good son, a good neighbor and a good lawyer.

She was in so much trouble on such an unexpectedly personal level. Every now and then, there was an awkward moment. A lingering look. A yearning glance. But they were adults. They'd controlled themselves.

The next time he invited her to go for a ride, attend a party or have a meal, she should say no. That would be best for both of them.

But she'd make sure she said goodbye before she drove off into the proverbial sunset. By Christmas Day, she should be basking in sunlight along the Pacific Ocean, sightseeing in Hollywood and finding a new apartment as close as she could afford to Diego's salon. Now, that would be the life, she told herself with just a bit of forced enthusiasm.

JAMES HAD TO GO to Graham for a meeting at the courthouse on Wednesday, so he took the opportunity to do a little Christmas shopping. There were several stores around the square that offered a variety of gift items his mother might like, plus he needed a few presents for aunts, uncles, cousins and his two nieces. His family had put a dollar limit on gifts years ago, and he'd always chafed at the ten-dollar restriction. But that's what worked best for everyone else, and he respected their rules. If he couldn't find what he needed around the square, though, he'd be forced to go to the big discount store down Highway 16. He'd rather spend his money with the local merchants.

The air felt brisk as he walked across the street. The businesses were decorated just like in Brody's Crossing. Graham, being the county seat, was a lot larger, plus they had a nice-size gazebo near the pale gray courthouse. A Confederate memorial stood out front, plus another veterans memorial off to the side. The place projected an aura of permanence, past oil wealth, and hope for the future despite occasional economic downturns.

As he entered a store that sold candles Aunt Mary might like, he saw a display of silver necklaces. Flashy and funky and fun, they reminded him of Scarlett. He stopped and ran several of them through his fingers, feeling the cool, smooth metal and thinking of her belly button ring. He would never make that little moon and star quiver as he ran his fingers along her waist, her stomach, her ribs. Her breasts.

James breathed deeply. He didn't want to think of Scarlett. He didn't want to imagine what they might do together, if only things were different.

No, that wasn't right. He *wanted* to think about her all the time. He just knew he shouldn't. There was no future with her, and he'd vowed that when he decided to get married again, he'd find someone from around the area who understood his feelings for his hometown and neighbors. The future Mrs. Brody would need to understand that he didn't want to move, become a big-city lawyer again.

So, Scarlett wasn't a woman he could build a future with. Intellectually, he realized that. For some reason, his body wasn't getting the message from his brain. He wanted her even though he knew she would be out of here as soon as her car was repaired. He wanted her even though he knew they were worlds apart in goals, temperament and style.

"May I help you?" the lady behind the counter asked.

James let the silver necklaces slip through his fingers. He smiled at the saleslady. "I'm looking for a candle for my aunt. One of those big, squatty ones in the glass jars."

"I know just what you mean. Right this way."

He walked down the aisle, but turned back to look one more time at the sparkling jewelry. Would Scarlett be here for Christmas? Should he buy her a gift?

"What fragrance does your aunt like?" the saleslady asked, bringing James's attention back to the task at hand.

"She likes flowers. She gardens."

He smelled about six different scents, settling on roses because he knew she liked them, and he really couldn't remember if tulips had any scent. He thought the candle maker might be cheating a little on that one.

The saleslady wrapped the candle in layers of paper and put it in a bag. The silver necklaces beckoned once more. *Should* he buy Scarlett a Christmas gift?

Closing his eyes, he decided to go for it. "I'll take this, also," he said, choosing a rather wild depiction of the sun that he thought might go with that pesky moon and star. The necklace would look good nestled between her breasts. He could imagine that sight even if he never saw it in person.

"Would you like a gift box for this?" the woman asked.

"Yes." If he didn't give it to Scarlett for Christmas, he could always present it to her as a going-away gift. Something for all those sunny, California days in her future. He was not cheered by the thought.

Obviously, Scarlett wasn't looking for anything permanent in Texas. Maybe she wouldn't mind a little fling. If he was willing to think only about this week, maybe the next, could they have a good time and part as friends? Why not? If they were honest with each other, no one would be hurt.

He could do this, he told himself as he headed into the next shop. He'd never vowed to wait like a monk for the future Mrs. Brody. He could enjoy Scarlett and let her go. She'd made her plans clear; now he needed to make his intentions obvious with a bold move.

ON WEDNESDAY Clarissa decided they'd close for lunch, since they didn't have any clients scheduled. Her friends had a meeting planned at the café, and she wanted everyone to attend—including Scarlett, who knew nothing about the subject matter, a farmers' market. Still, they insisted, so she headed off for lunch with Venetia and Clarissa to meet Ida Bell, Raven York and Bobbi Jean Maxwell.

To Scarlett's surprise, James's mother came through the door a moment after they'd sat down. Scarlett didn't know how she felt about spending time with the mother of the man she lusted after.

"The grand opening of the farmers' market is scheduled for March 15," Ida Bell said after they'd ordered lunch. "We need something really spectacular to involve all the merchants downtown."

They started with ideas for themes and tie-ins for the different businesses. Scarlett got much more involved than she thought she would, imagining how the new market for plants, herbs, fruits, vegetables, nuts and assorted crafts would impact Brody's Crossing. She thought of something a salon she'd worked at a few years ago had participated in, and hesitated only briefly before jumping in.

"How about a scavenger hunt, or some other kind of

activity, where people need to go to a number of businesses to get something or have something signed?"

"That's a great idea!" Clarissa said. "I love scavenger hunts and no one has them anymore. We could all provide something very inexpensive for the asking."

"And I'll bet the bank would give us some of those plastic tote bags with their logo on them for people to put the items in," Bobbi Jean said.

They worked out details and a list of possible giveaways. Everyone wanted Scarlett to head up this effort, until she reminded them that she would be leaving town next week, as soon as her car was repaired. By March 15 she would be settled in L.A.

"But what are you doing for Christmas? Surely you're not spending it all alone, in a strange town," Ida exclaimed.

"I need a little time to get acclimated. My new job starts January 2, and I have to find an apartment. I probably won't get to do much celebrating this year, but the move will be worth it."

"Well, I know, but it seems so lonely."

"She'll be fine," Clarissa said, "although we'll miss her like crazy."

Scarlett felt touched that the other ladies seemed really sad. Truthfully, she was a bit sad also. The grand opening sounded like fun. They talked about a few more events, then finished their pie and coffee and adjourned the meeting. They all decided to meet after the New Year to finalize the plans.

When she started her job in L.A., Scarlett would be assisting another stylist. She'd have to play gopher and earn the respect of others. But she'd at least be someplace where she would be appreciated for being innovative. She wouldn't be constantly criticized for not living up to expectations.

She, Clarissa and Venetia walked back to the salon,

ready to get to work again. Scarlett felt very much a part
of the town today, but knew it was an illusion. Even if she
made the ridiculous choice to stay in Brody's Crossing—
which had zero chance of happening because of her great
opportunity in California—she knew this sense of cama-
raderie wouldn't last. She wasn't sure why, but nothing
good seemed to, no matter how much you wanted it to.

No, it was best to move on before people got tired of
her or she got tired of the place. Next week would be soon
enough. But she would miss this town, these people.

She would miss James Brody, too, but she didn't want
to think about that.

AT THE END OF THE DAY, as she cleaned up her station,
Scarlett heard the door open, and looked up to see James.

"Hi there, hon," Clarissa greeted him as she completed
the deposit slip for the cash and checks in the drawer. "We
were just closing up, so I'm glad you're here. I have to run
to the bank and you can keep Scarlett company."

"I can do that." At his smile, Scarlett looked away.

Clarissa zipped up the bag. "You two young people
have fun."

Scarlett's head snapped up. What was Clarissa thinking,
making suggestive remarks? James seemed amused by her
words. Scarlett wondered why that roused such different
emotions in her. She wanted to volunteer to take the deposit
to the bank, to run away from James. On the other hand,
she really wanted to have fun, lots of fun, even though she
knew she shouldn't find him entertaining. She grabbed a
broom and dustpan instead.

"My mother said you came up with a good idea at the
farmers' market meeting today," he said, settling in one of
the chairs across from her station. He stretched out his

long legs, covered in neatly pressed chinos, and crossed his feet. His shoes were polished and his socks matched his dark brown sweater, worn over a button-down plaid shirt. Today, he appeared superpreppy, even with his adorably ruffled hair.

"I tried to help. The farmers' market idea sounds like a good one." She swept under the chair with gusto.

"I think so. People can get fresh produce, and it gives farmers and crafters a place to sell their goods locally."

And *locally* was all-important to James. "How are the Holmeses? Any progress with the money-grubbing nephew?"

"I've contacted his attorney. I think he'll get the message." James shifted in the chair.

Scarlett could find nothing else to sweep, so she put the broom and dustpan in the long cabinet. "Well, I guess I'm all cleaned up. Time to lock up."

"I think Clarissa did that on the way out."

"Oh." Scarlett felt alarmed that she'd missed the fact that she and James were locked in. Of course, there was a very large window about twelve feet to her left. Anyone could see in, so what mischief could occur? Not that she wanted anything to happen.

"Do you have any plans for dinner?"

"There's a tuna salad sandwich that Venetia brought for lunch and didn't eat." Which sounded even less appealing than it looked.

James grimaced. "How about a home-cooked meal?"

"Whose home?" she asked, thinking of his mother.

"Mine."

"Is your mom cooking?"

"No, I am."

"Oh," Scarlett said, and frowned. "Don't you live with your parents?"

"No! Where did you get that idea?"

"I...I have no idea. I just assumed, since you never talked about your own place, that you lived at their ranch, where we drove that day."

"No. I have an apartment over the office. It's a lot more convenient."

She thought back to the time he'd admitted seeing her in the little memorial park. She hadn't realized he meant from his apartment, upstairs.

He stood and walked to where she stood against the cabinet. "So, do you want to try my cooking? I'm not bad, if I do say so myself. A meal at my place will beat an old tuna salad sandwich, that's for sure."

"You have a point." She faced another night of country-and-western music or staticky vintage rock. She had nothing to do, very little to read and a real urge to discover what single, preppy men from small Texas towns would consider home cooking for a female friend. "Okay."

"Great. Are you ready now? Do you need to...do anything?"

"No, I'm finished, unless you think I should change." She held out her arms. She wore jeans and her green sweater—again. She was really tired of the same clothes, but she hadn't packed a lot of cold-weather choices. California was warm and sunny most of the time. She hadn't expected to need heavy sweaters and boots except for the drive out to L.A.

"No, you look great, as usual."

Scarlett chuckled. "You're probably tired of seeing me in the same clothes."

James scanned her, head to toe and smiled. "That's one way of looking at it."

Scarlett wondered why she couldn't think of double en-tendres before she opened her mouth and inserted her foot.

"Come on, preppy boy. We'll go out the back so I can lock that door."

"Sounds good. After you," he said, sweeping his arm toward her temporary living quarters.

She got the impression he was looking at *her* backside rather than the old sofa, posters and kitchen area. She grabbed her hoodie and hurried toward the door before either one of them said anything that could be interpreted as more than friendly.

JAMES PLACED THE SECOND thick pork chop on Scarlett's plate and spooned a little of the drippings over it. He hoped she enjoyed his cooking. He didn't have a large culinary repertoire, but he'd learned to fix meals in college. He made his own dinner a couple of times a week.

"It's nice to have someone to cook for," he said as he placed the plates on the small table near the back door. His kitchen overlooked the little park. There was a small landing and a metal staircase that led downstairs.

"Everything smells delicious," she said.

James looked down at her before taking his seat. She appeared wide-eyed with anticipation. For his cooking, or something else? He was projecting his own desire, he knew, but as usual had little control over his thoughts of Scarlett.

He sat down fast so she wouldn't see her effect on his body. "Dig in," he invited, reaching for the bottle of pinot noir. He added a little to both their glasses.

"Believe me, I will. I can't believe how hungry I am for home cooking." She cut a piece of pork chop, then popped it into her mouth. He almost groaned when she closed her eyes and moaned in bliss.

"My mother makes pork chops," she said, "but not these thick ones. These are good."

"We have a new butcher in town. I have him cut them thick and trim off the fat." *Geesh, James, could you talk about anything more romantic than trimming pork chops?* "I hope you like steamed vegetables." *Yeah, that's a lot more romantic.* "Bread?" he asked, pushing the basket toward her.

"Thanks, and yes, I like the vegetables, too." She smiled at him, and he didn't feel quite as awkward. He dug into his own meal and decided he really was a pretty good cook.

"Do you cook?" he asked her.

"Not really. I lived at home most of the time, and my mother didn't want me to bother with cooking." Scarlett shook her head. "Either that, or she didn't want to be bothered with someone else messing up her kitchen. Basically, she fixed the food and we ate it."

"I'll bet you miss some of the meals, though."

Scarlett shrugged. "Maybe. I'm going to kind of miss Christmas dinner. Mom makes this really good stuffing with sausage and apples and lots of sage. And she gets a smoked turkey from this place—I'm not sure where, but it comes in a foam cooler with dry ice—and we eat every bite of that bird."

"Sounds yummy. You should get the dressing recipe."

"Why? I don't cook, remember?" she replied with a grin, then plopped a slice of carrot in her mouth.

I'll cook for you, he wanted to say, but didn't. He shouldn't put pressure on her. If he didn't talk about her leaving, and she didn't say anything about it, then maybe it wouldn't happen too soon. Maybe she'd decide that Brody's Crossing would be a good place to spend Christmas, and they could have a great time for a while.

They finished their meal, and then Scarlett reached for the plates. "Let me, since you cooked."

"I have a dishwasher."

"I'll rinse then, and you load."

They stood side by side at the sink, bumping elbows and shoulders, until James felt as if he'd explode. He wanted to throw the dishes on the floor, grab Scarlett and kiss her senseless. But he wasn't going to do that. He had more finesse than grabbing and groping a woman he'd invited to dinner.

Didn't he?

He took a deep breath. She bumped hips with him. On purpose. "What was that for?"

She laughed, the sound foreign in his apartment. "Just because. We seem to be in each other's way."

"Maybe we shouldn't fight it."

"Fight it?" She stilled, wiped her hands on a dish towel and pivoted to face him. "What do you mean?"

He turned toward her, then reached out and took her soft, slightly damp hands in his. "We're attracted to each other. We fight it. Then we tell each other that we're just friends."

She nodded, swallowed, but didn't pull away. "Seems like our M.O. What are you suggesting?"

"I'm saying that despite what we say, despite what we think we *should* do, we're still attracted." He gently pulled her closer. "Maybe we shouldn't fight the feelings. Maybe we should listen to our bodies instead of heeding all that conventional wisdom."

She placed her hands on his waist and leaned closer, looking up. The overhead light made her eyes sparkle— with mischief or something else, he couldn't tell. "I was never good with conventional wisdom, anyway."

He smiled. "I'm terrific with all the traditional thinking, clichés and societal norms. I'm also getting better at ignoring those things that simply don't work in a given situation."

"This being a 'given situation'?" she asked, her voice husky and so darn sexy he about grabbed her and ran for the bedroom.

"Exactly," he whispered, before he bent down and kissed her.

Scarlett wound her arms around his waist, leaned into him and gave herself over to the kiss. Oh, that man could kiss. His lips molded to hers, his tongue thrust sure and strong, and she couldn't get enough.

His body was tall and lean and so incredibly warm. She wanted to crawl inside his skin. She wanted to be absorbed by his heat and passion.

"James," she whispered as he kissed his way to the side of her neck.

"Umm," he murmured, but said nothing else. He was obviously too busy, and as soon as he hit that spot just below her ear, she didn't really want to talk, either.

"Would you like to see the rest of the apartment now?" he asked as his hands roamed close to her breasts.

"Now?" she breathed. What was left to see? Why did she have to open her eyes, anyway?

"Um, I think the only room you haven't seen is my bedroom." Her eyes opened, unfocused. His hands stilled and he looked down at her. "What do you think?"

"How far is it?" she whispered, pulling him close again.

"Not too far, thank heavens," he murmured. He cupped her bottom, lifted her and started walking.

Scarlett bent her knees and looped her legs around his waist, bringing her right up against that part of him that felt so very good. "Walking is good for your heart," she whispered into his ear, "and it feels really, really wonderful."

He chuckled and boosted her a little higher. "Our exercise has just begun," he said before reaching a dark room that she assumed was the aforementioned bedroom. Yep, she thought as he eased her backward until she lay on a high, wide mattress.

She reluctantly removed her legs from around his waist. Looking about, she said, "Nice room." Not that she could really see anything, since the only light came down the hall from the front rooms. "Now, where were we?"

"Joined at the hip?"

"Oh, yes." That had felt really, really great. "Tell me you are prepared, because I—"

He placed a finger on her sensitive lips. "Don't worry. I know all about being ready for any contingency."

"Of course you do," she said, pulling him down so she could nibble on his neck for a change.

Now that they were in his bedroom and on the bed, and he'd answered the question correctly, Scarlett sensed the change in James. She felt it also. The time for talking had passed. The time for teasing was over. Her eyes adjusted to the darkness. She saw his face, his intense expression, his wide shoulders. Pale light threaded through the dark brown strands of his hair, and her fingers followed, shaping it into slight spikes and smoothing it down again.

His hands learned her body and she arched toward him, her breath catching at the sheer excitement of making love with James. And they hadn't even removed their clothes yet. As soon as she formed the thought, his fingers began to ease her sweater up, over her rib cage, over the demi-cups of her bright pink bra. She raised off the bed a little and he removed the sweater.

He was so neat that she half expected him to fold it, but instead, he flung it away. Scarlett smiled. She loved James's rare, uncharacteristic actions.

"Whoever said pink and red clash never saw your underwear," he said with near reverence. "Wow."

"I do like underwear."

"I like *your* underwear."

"I'd like to see yours now."

Chapter Eight

"In a moment. There's something I must do right now."

She propped herself up on her elbows and watched, amused and aroused, as he carefully unbuttoned and unzipped her jeans. Fortunately, she'd worn matching panties today. He removed her half-boots and long socks, which weren't sexy at all. Her feet, however, were darn cute. She'd painted her toenails a cheerful red and placed a twinkling crystal on both big toes with clear topcoat.

She lifted her hips as he slid the jeans off, the rasp of denim making her feel even more feminine and vulnerable. He threw them in the general direction of her sweater.

"I've wanted to do this from the first moment I saw you, standing in Clarissa's salon," he said. With that, he lifted her toward the center of the big bed, and she sank into the thick comforter. He stretched out over her, his hands just above her waist, almost but not quite touching her breasts.

Then he leaned down and she felt his hot, damp breath on her stomach. His tongue flicked out and teased her belly button ring. He played with the little charms, kissed and sucked all around there until he had to hold her still or she would have wiggled off the bed.

"Stop," she called weakly. She couldn't stand any more. And yet she wanted more. Much more.

"That is so cool," he said, grinning up at her. His grin faded as his attention caught on her pink bra. *Yes*, she felt like shouting.

He worked the front clasp as if he knew exactly what he was doing. He peeled the cups back, then moved up her body. *Yes, right there*, she wanted to cry, but her breath left her as she collapsed on the bed. *I should be doing something*, she thought as he eased her panties off. But she was too enthralled by what James was doing to her. *Next time*, she silently promised as she helped him lose her underwear to the shadowy corner.

The night became a blur. He moved over her. He momentarily shifted away and she knew he was donning a condom. He eased into her body, then stilled, held her head between his hands and kissed her tenderly. Tears welled in her eyes from the sweetness of the moment. Never, ever had she felt as she did right now. She kissed James back, wound her arms around him, held him tight as he began to move. Slowly, then faster as she collapsed to the bed and watched the dim light swirl around them.

Then soon, far too soon but not nearly soon enough, the colors of a million Christmas lights centered behind her eyes and exploded inside her head. She cried out and held on to James, felt him shudder and stiffen in her arms, and sank into the darkness.

JAMES AWOKE TO HEAR A BIRD chirping in one of the small trees in the park outside his bedroom window. Darn bird. It often woke him before dawn. He grabbed his extra pillow and rolled over—and encountered a warm, petite body.

The night rushed back to him. This wasn't just any

morning; this was the morning after the night he and Scarlett had made love. How could he have forgotten that for even a minute? Even sleep-deprived and groggy?

He rolled fully to his side, propped himself up on one elbow and smiled. She lay on her stomach, her head turned toward him. Even in the predawn darkness, he could see her bright red hair, more spiked than usual. He remembered that although it appeared firm, it was very soft when he ran his hands through it. When he held her head and kissed her until they were both breathless.

Thinking about Scarlett had the usual effect on him: he was ready to make love again. And again. Unfortunately, she was still asleep, and he didn't want to wake her this early. They hadn't slept all that much the night before.

Of course, he rationalized, they had gone to bed early—right after dinner dishes. So perhaps they had gotten seven or eight hours of sleep, broken up by making love two times during the night.

He leaned over and kissed her cheek, which was the only sensible place he could reach, since she was covered to her neck with a sheet and comforter. If he remembered correctly, she had nothing on under the covers. Neither did he. Convenient. He smiled again and watched her stir.

"Is it morning?" she asked in a sleepy, husky voice.

"Technically. It's not dawn yet."

"Um, that's good," she replied, snuggling closer. "You're so warm."

He put his arms around her, pulling her tight against his hot, aroused body. "Are you ready to get even warmer?"

She wiggled a little. Her breasts settled against his chest. One of her legs wrapped over his hip. "Maybe."

"Are we into negotiations? I'm pretty good at that, being a lawyer and all."

"Umm. How about you be quiet and let me get to work?"

He felt a moment of acute disappointment. She was leaving? Right now? But then she pressed him onto his back, straddled him, and pulled the comforter over both of them. Darn. He couldn't see her body now.

He forgot that minor complaint when she reached between them and found him, already at attention.

"Condom?" she said, husky but no longer sleepy sounding.

He reached toward the nightstand, handed her one and held his breath as she tore it open and rolled it on. Oh, yes. He sucked in air and moaned at the same time.

He felt more than saw Scarlett's smile. *Wicked hussy,* he thought with a grin. She settled over him, took him into her body and had her way with him. Oh, that woman could move. He grabbed her hips, held on tight and let the feelings of *rightness* rush through him, followed some time later by one fantastic climax.

"You've ruined me for other women," he whispered into her hair as she panted against his chest.

Again, he felt her smile, but then she pushed away.

"I need to go," she said.

SCARLETT DIDN'T EXACTLY panic when she realized dawn was breaking, but she did hurry. She needed to be back at the salon before people were up and about. She wouldn't be responsible for ruining the reputation of one very upstanding attorney.

She ungracefully "dismounted" from James, slid from beneath the very warm comforter and headed for the pile of clothes. Last night she'd been amused that he'd flung them away, but he had good aim. Her underwear, sweater and jeans were piled so she could reach down, grab them and dash to the bathroom.

She washed quickly, used her finger and his toothpaste to "brush," donned her clothes, and ran her fingers through her wild hair. There. She was as ready as she was going to get without a hot shower and makeup.

She opened the bathroom door to find a naked James leaning against the frame. "Eek!" she shrieked before she could stop herself. Apparently, she was a little more nervous than she'd thought.

"Let me in for a minute, then I'll get dressed and walk you back to the salon."

"No! You can't."

"Of course I can. It's not fully light yet, and I wouldn't feel right letting you walk alone."

"This is Brody's Crossing, not Atlanta. Or L.A."

"I know. That doesn't change how I would feel about you leaving alone, though," he said, brushing past her into the bathroom.

She hadn't thought of it that way. She didn't want to answer questions about where she'd been, what she'd been doing or who she'd been doing it with. *Especially* who she'd been doing it with.

She went into the kitchen and found her hoodie. The kitchen window faced west, so she couldn't see the sunrise, but the sky was lightening to gray, increasing her sense of panic. She had a perm scheduled for ten o'clock. She needed to grab a shower, get composed, before then.

As she looked around the kitchen for anything she might have missed, she wondered if James was sorry that they'd slept together. Did he regret inviting her to dinner? He'd obviously enjoyed himself. At least three times, if she remembered correctly, but that didn't mean he was happy about having a—what? They weren't having an affair, were they? That was so old-fashioned! And they'd done more than hook up, since they'd discussed the whole friends and more-than-friends thing. Maybe they were friends-with-benefits. That was modern and uncomplicated, right?

"I'll be ready to walk you home in just a minute," he said from the other room.

She had to hurry! She didn't want to go, but she had to get back to the salon before the town awakened. And she didn't correct him, but the salon wasn't "home," and never would be.

With a soft click, she unlocked the door and slipped out into the cold morning.

SCARLETT KNEW THEY'D BEEN lucky this morning; no one had seen her slip in the back door. At least, no one she *knew* of. She was pretty sure that if anyone saw her, she'd hear about it before noon, she thought as she pulled off her clothes in the small bathroom.

She wouldn't do anything to hurt James's reputation. After all, it just wouldn't do for a future judge to be seen cavorting with the town's redheaded stranger. She ruffled her hair in the mirror. Was it time for a change? Would James like her hair another way? Another color?

She jumped into the shower. Oh, why was she thinking about what he would like? She'd always done what *she* wanted with her hair. With every aspect of her life. In near record time, she'd washed away the evidence of their night together. If only she could get rid of the doubts just as easily, she thought as she dried herself.

Her normal reaction to inherent criticism was to flaunt her acts in the face of moral outrage. She tossed the towel in the hamper and reached for her clothes.

She couldn't imagine doing such a thing to James. Which meant…what? She slowly pulled a stretchy, white, long-sleeved T-shirt over her head as comprehension dawned. Oh, no. She'd begun to care way too much for James Brody. Way, way too much. She was half in love with him already. She'd only known him a week and a half! How could she be falling in love with him that quickly? How could she do something so incredibly stupid?

She felt a renewed sense of panic, as if she needed to escape out the door, run fast and hard and never look back. This wasn't her home. This wasn't where she was supposed to be. She needed to get to Los Angeles, to Diego's nice salon, where she had a future.

Why would she put herself through the aggravation of comb-outs on cranky women who had too-tight perms? Getting criticism for not executing updos on unsuspecting teens? Being threatened by blue-haired ladies for daring to update their color and style?

For James, a tiny voice said, and she felt even more panic. She didn't want to love someone when she couldn't be herself! She was Scarlett! She was independent and self-confident and talented. She wouldn't settle for working in a small-town salon when she had the break—when she'd *made* the opportunity—to become a stylist to the stars.

By the time she was dressed, her hair and makeup done, the acute panic had settled down to a milder urge to run. She needed to get to L.A. Somehow.

Clarissa unlocked the front door and entered with a cheerful smile, wearing a bright Christmas sweater, black knit slacks and dangling ornament earrings. She immediately reached for a pink smock. Scarlett took one look at her and saw her future. The urge to run returned.

"Clarissa," she said, rushing toward the older woman, "tell me how I can get out of town. Fast."

JAMES FROWNED as his mother talked about the farmers' market grand opening. He'd been reading a recent court ruling that could relate to the case before the bench in Graham, and was now staring out the window at the bare limbs of trees in the park and watching birds search for tiny red berries among the green bushes. He was not in the Christmas spirit.

"James, what's going on?" his mother had asked as she came into his office right before lunch. "You look angry and you're late for lunch."

"Sorry." He couldn't very well tell her that Scarlett had run out on him before he'd zipped his jeans this morning. His parents weren't overly judgmental and wouldn't be shocked if he told them he'd had sex outside of marriage. Surely they didn't think he'd been celibate since his divorce.

Come to think of it, he had lived like a monk most of the time. There was one weekend where he and a former college girlfriend had gone to Dallas for a Mavericks game, dinner and hotel stay. But for the most part, he'd been busy with his new law practice. Besides, he didn't want to flaunt a relationship. He especially didn't want to give any single women in Brody's Crossing the impression that he could be serious about them. He wasn't ready to look for the future Mrs. Brody, and he didn't know of anyone locally who made him think of marrying again.

"James, you're acting very strange." His mother placed her palm on his forehead. "You might be running a little fever."

You're so warm, Scarlett had said before she'd strad-dled his body.

"Um, I'd better get to lunch," he murmured. "Are you eating in or going to the café?"

"I'm meeting some friends there. Why?"

"You go ahead. I'll lock up in a minute when I leave."

"Are you sure you don't want me to take your temperature? Maybe you have a cold."

"No, really, I'm fine. Just go to lunch. I'll see you in a little while."

He had a decision to make: how to confront a woman who'd walked out on him. He'd never done that before, had never been in this situation. Before Scarlett, he couldn't have imagined wanting to talk to a woman who'd run away from him.

Ignoring Scarlett wasn't an option, he thought as he picked up the phone.

"Er, no, Scarlett can't come to the phone right now," Venetia said as Scarlett stood behind her client, frantically shaking her head. She assumed her eyes appeared wild and wide.

"Sure, I'll tell her you called. Have a nice day." Venetia hung up and frowned at her. "Now, why wouldn't you want to talk to him?"

"I'm busy," she said, looking down at the salt-and-pepper curls of her ten o'clock perm, cut and style.

"Hmm. Too busy for J—"

"Yes! I'll call him back."

Venetia shook her head, but returned to her station.

Scarlett knew she should act normally, as if she hadn't spent the night with James. But darn it, she wasn't that good an actress. She was, however, good at drama. And she was basically an honest person.

She would call James back before she left town. Clarissa was off working on that right now, bless her heart. She'd gone to the café for lunch, and promised she'd keep her ears open in case she heard any juicy rumors.

Scarlett finished styling and spraying her client, accepted a thank-you and a tip, and rushed to the back of the salon. Taking a deep breath, she wet a washcloth and pressed it to her toasty face.

You're so warm, she remembered telling James just hours ago as she'd snuggled against his hot, aroused body. The memory made her cheeks burn and her eyes water. Maybe she was coming down with something other than acute infatuation.

Before she could wallow in her emotions, the front door opened and she heard Clarissa's cheerful voice greet Venetia. Scarlett folded the washcloth, took a calming breath and went out to greet her boss. Her friend.

"How are you, hon?" Clarissa asked, removing her coat and taking Scarlett's hands.

"I'm okay. Well, not okay, but I'm getting by. Did you learn anything?"

"The good news is that there's no gossip going around, so whatever you were worried about isn't a problem. The bad news is there's a bus leaving tonight, but not around here. Weatherford. That's the closest city, but it's over an hour's drive in the daylight."

"Oh." That threw a wrench into her plans for a clean escape. "Where's Weatherford, exactly?"

"You go through Graham, down to Mineral Wells and then on to Weatherford. It's about thirty miles west of Fort Worth, right off Interstate 20."

"But how would I get there?"

Clarissa took a big breath and perched on the edge of the couch. "Well, I suppose I could drive you," she offered, although Scarlett figured it was a reluctant proposal.

She couldn't ask James, Scarlett knew. Not after she'd realized she was a hair width away from falling in love with him. Her cheeks felt hot again and she began to pace.

"There's one other option," Clarissa said. "Bobbi Jean Maxwell is selling her van. Now, it's not new, but she's kept it up real nice." Clarissa frowned. "Except for that unfortunate incident when Raven got accused of being a cattle rustler and that calf had a little accident in the back. But, really, that's minor, and they cleaned it up."

Scarlett felt as if she should shake her head to clear the image of cattle rustling and calf accidents. "What kind of van, did you say?"

"It's a 1987 model, teal-blue, with a bed that folds out from the seating area in the back. There are even little wood cabinets and a built-in cooler, and this nice desert scene painted on the side."

"Uh, sounds nice." For the eighties, maybe. "But I doubt it gets very good gas mileage, and besides, I can't afford to buy anything."

"Well, I told her I'd mention it to you."

"Thanks, Clarissa." Scarlett sagged against the arm of the couch. "I just don't know what to do."

"Hon, it's probably none of my business, but can you tell me why you feel like you have to leave right now? Today? I thought your stay here was going well."

"I…I just realized some things."

"Did any of us do something to upset you?"

"No! Not at all. Everyone has been…great." That was true. People in Brody's Crossing had been very friendly this week. Even the saloon girl costume hadn't put them off.

"Then it must be James."

"What?" Scarlett stepped back from the couch, feeling sudden panic again. "Why did you say that?"

"If everything else is fine, it must be a man. And hon, from what I've seen between you and James, he's the man."

"He didn't do anything."

Clarissa looked at her, her perfectly penciled eyebrows raised. "It takes two to tango. I haven't been widowed so long that I've forgotten that."

"What if you really liked to dance with someone and you knew you shouldn't?" Scarlett asked carefully.

Clarissa didn't answer for a moment, and about the time she opened her mouth, Venetia entered the back and announced, "Clarissa, your one o'clock is here."

She pushed herself up from the sofa. "Gotta go, hon. I'll think about that question. In the meantime, why don't you think about talking to you-know-who about whether you should catch that bus."

Clarissa walked out to her station. Venetia frowned at Scarlett. "What bus?"

"I thought…maybe I shouldn't wait for my car. Maybe it won't be fixed. Maybe I should just leave."

Venetia's frown turned more intense. "Why in the world would you leave? It's Christmastime, and things are going so well."

Venetia shook her head and left as Scarlett plopped down on the couch. She couldn't work up any enthusiasm to move. Should she pack up her bags and ask Clarissa to drive her to Weatherford? When should she talk to James?

And if he asked her to stay, then what? Avoid James and protect her heart? Accept the attraction and sneak around? Tango in the dark?

She didn't have answers because she'd never been in this situation before.

Clarissa walked back a minute later. "Look, I know I shouldn't interfere, but I don't think you should rush off. At least, not tonight. Think about your options for a while. In the meantime, come with us to the chili supper at the VFW Post. It will get your mind off you-know-who."

"I don't think I'd be good company."

"You'll be fine, and if you don't come, you'll be sitting here all alone. Or maybe you'll be with James," Clarissa said, raising her penciled brows once more. "Trying to convince him that the two of you aren't good together."

Scarlett groaned and buried her face in her hands. "That's so not fair."

"Fair or not, it's the truth."

"I don't even like chili."

"You'll like this chili," Clarissa said, taking her arm and tugging her to her feet. "It's real Texas chili, not that imitation stuff with the beans or, Lord forbid, spaghetti. Why, that's nearly a sacrilege!"

Scarlett couldn't help but smile despite her dour mood. "Where is the VFW Post?"

"It's on the highway that goes to Olney. The chili supper is a tradition. The vets and their families are just about the best people around."

"I've never been to a VFW before."

"Then it's high time you went," Clarissa said. "We'll close the shop at five o'clock sharp, run by the grocery and head on out."

Scarlett shrugged. "I'm obviously at your mercy."

Chapter Nine

James hadn't heard from Scarlett, although he'd called several times. He wasn't sure if he should be alarmed or angry. She had no reason to steer clear of him, just as she'd had no reason to walk out on him this morning. They'd had a great time. Neither one of them had put pressure on the other.

So, maybe she was busy. He had a late meeting, but as soon as his clients left, he grabbed his jacket and walked down to the salon.

The multicolored lights surrounding Clarissa's big picture window blinked in the dusky twilight, but the salon appeared dark inside. James glanced at his watch. Not even a quarter after five. He knocked on the door, thinking Scarlett might be in the back, but she didn't answer.

Now he was getting concerned. He walked around the building, noting there were no cars in the parking lot. When he stepped onto the little porch and knocked on the back door, she didn't answer.

She wasn't here. She hadn't called him. What was going on?

On a hunch, he walked across the street, past the Burger Barn and onto the asphalt parking area of McCaskie's garage. Scarlett's white Mercedes was parked off to the side, the hood open. The car looked as if it had been gutted, the interior dark and smoky-black. Very sad.

Well, one thing was certain; she hadn't driven herself out of town. So where was she?

WHEN JAMES ENTERED the Crawford-Peet VFW Post just out of town, his senses were assaulted by the smells of chili, beer and old cigarette smoke. His eyes took in the huge Christmas tree with its big red, white and blue lights, yellow ribbons tied in big bows and many ornaments, and he heard George Strait singing Christmas carols over the speaker system.

The place was packed for the annual chili dinner. Where was Scarlett? Hopefully with Clarissa, Venetia and the "gang," and not with a rangy cowboy or a buff vet, who might sweep her off her feet.

He couldn't believe he felt jealous of an imaginary rival. There was no evidence Scarlett was looking for anyone else to spend time with.

Of course, he'd felt the same when she'd talked about Diego, until he'd figured out that ol' Diego probably wasn't interested in Scarlett *that* way.

James made his way through the crowd, greeting a half-dozen neighbors and clients he knew. Every stool at the bar was taken, but not by Scarlett. He headed for the buffet table. There, at the end, stood Clarissa and Ida Bell, chatting away. They'd know where Scarlett was.

He headed for the ladies. "Sorry to interrupt, but is Scarlett with you?"

"Hello, James. Yes, she is. She's around here somewhere," Clarissa said, standing on her tiptoes.

He looked around again, then frowned.

"She's fine, in case you're worried." Clarissa leaned close and whispered, "I don't know what happened between the two of you, but she was pretty upset."

"I honestly don't know why."

The woman leaned back a little and shook her head. "Son, men never do."

"There she is," Ida said, waving toward the buffet table.

He looked across the room and saw Scarlett, a cup of chili in her hand, taking to some people he didn't know. She looked…fine. Smiling, gesturing. Not worried, injured, sick or anything. Instead of being relieved, he felt…angry. Narrowing his eyes, he headed toward her.

"We need to talk," he said. The other people scurried off.

"Okay," she said, holding up the cup of chili. "This is surprisingly good."

"Not about the chili."

"Oh."

He looked around the crowded post. "How about outside?"

"I'm not sure. I need to check with my chaperone to see if that's okay."

"Very clever. I've already talked to Clarissa. She knows I'm here," he said, taking Scarlett's arm and steering her toward the front door. Fortunately, she decided to cooperate. Unlike this morning, he reminded himself.

"Where are we going?"

"My car. It's the only place to sit out of the wind."

"I'm not sure I want to be in the car with you."

"Tough. You should have thought about that when you ran out this morning."

"Darn it, James, I—"

She started to walk in the wrong direction, so he pulled her toward his SUV. "I'm not used to women running away from me."

"Oh, sorry. I didn't know you had such a fragile ego."

"I don't have a fragile ego. I do, however, have a sense of what's right and wrong."

"Oh, and I don't?"

He unlocked the doors, then opened the passenger side. "I want to understand what happened. Why."

Scarlett sighed. "Can't we just say we each had a good time, and move on?"

He came around to his side of the SUV, opened the door and sat down. In the stillness of the parked car, he turned to her and said, "Apparently not. Believe me, I'm kind of surprised, too."

He must have shocked her, because she had no snappy comeback. Instead, she looked down at her hands, still holding the cup of chili. He decided not to say anything else, let her gather her thoughts.

Finally, she said, "I guess I panicked."

"You guess?"

"Okay, I did." She placed the cup on the dash and turned to him. "I didn't want anyone to see you with me."

"Why? I'm a big boy. I can take care of myself."

"But you were concerned before about what people saw us together. You're going to serve as a judge, for goodness sake. I didn't want to hurt your reputation."

"Scarlett, you're not really a saloon girl. You're not something negative I need to hide."

She shrugged. "I panicked, okay? I didn't say it was totally rational, but those are my actual reasons."

"You should think this through again. I'm not ashamed of you."

She sighed. "I'll think about it."

"I was angry when I thought about you running out on me this morning. Then I got worried when you didn't talk to me. I went to the salon after my last appointment, but it was closed up. I even went to the garage, but I couldn't find you."

"Oh." She frowned. "I had no idea you were looking for me that hard."

"Yeah, well, I was." And he wasn't real happy about it, either. Scarlett was not an easy woman to…what? Be involved with? But how long could he be involved with her when she was leaving as soon as possible?

"I thought about leaving. Now."

"What?"

"I'm…I'm having second thoughts about the new engine. About fixing the Benz." She looked out the side window. "Maybe it's not worth the money. And it's taking forever." She took a deep breath and hugged her arms tighter around herself. "I'm thinking of leaving the car here, maybe selling it or giving it to Claude in exchange for the cost of the engine, and getting out to L.A. another way."

"How?"

"A bus, maybe," she said in a small voice, not meeting James's eyes as he watched her. "Clarissa looked into schedules for me. I'd have to get to Weatherford. She talked me out of leaving tonight."

He felt stunned. Blindsided. "Tonight?"

Scarlett looked up at him and frowned. "I need to get to my new job."

"Right now?"

"Not this week, but I have to be in L.A. on January 2, when the salon reopens after the holidays. I got to thinking that maybe I don't need my car. If I went to L.A. early, I could find a place close to the salon, or on a bus route. I'd actually save money, because I wouldn't have to pay for parking or insurance or gas."

"You told me how you feel about that car. I can't believe you'd go off and leave it on a whim. Which makes me think whatever happened this morning wasn't a whim, it was important, and I'd like to understand."

"I… Well, I'm just not good at handling that panicky feeling."

"Who is? I had no idea I made you panic. I didn't realize how panicked I'd feel when I couldn't find you this afternoon. I'm sorry if I made you run away."

"It's not your fault. It's just…sometimes I feel as if… well, it *is* all too much."

"And you want to run as fast as you can."

"Get myself out of the situation," she corrected.

"That's equivocation."

"You're using those big lawyer words again."

He frowned at her. "Don't think I'm going to let you change the subject by putting yourself down."

"How can pointing out that you're a lawyer put *me* down?"

"When you make a disparaging remark about yourself."

"I didn't."

"You implied that my vocabulary is better than yours, because I have a degree you don't have."

"Hey, I have a degree. From cosmetology school."

He rolled his eyes and leaned his head back against the seat. "I can't have a conversation with you if you won't be honest."

She fell silent for a moment, then said, "I never lied to you."

"Maybe not, but you keep things from me."

"Like what?"

"Like what you're really thinking. How you really feel."

"Wait. Am I having a conversation with a guy or with my best girlfriend?"

"Very funny, Scarlett. I'm trying to understand you."

"Well, don't. I won't be here long enough for you to figure out all my problems."

"Oh, Scarlett. What am I going to do with you?"

She sighed. "You could get me a large latte with extra foam."

"And that will make you happy?"

"Ecstatic."

He shook his head and sighed. "I'm not sure about a latte, but I might be able to get you a cappuccino."

"That'll do."

He started the engine. "Do you need anything from inside?"

"No, everything is in my pockets."

He pulled out onto the highway, then headed southeast.

"Where are we going?" Scarlett asked. "I hadn't noticed anything like a Starbucks."

"There's a place on Highway 114. It's not exactly a coffee shop, but it'll do."

SCARLETT SETTLED BACK into the seat of James's SUV in the parking lot of the Valero gas station and convenience store. The cappuccino smelled great and was plenty hot.

"This was a surprise," she said as he settled into his seat and picked up his cup.

"Now, tell me more about this sudden desire to leave town, just about the time things got real interesting between us."

Interesting? That's how he described their night together?

Intense. Not unexpected, given their attraction. Inconvenient. That's how she'd describe it.

"A while ago, you said I wasn't being honest with you, but I always said I was leaving as soon as I could get my car fixed. I need this chance to be successful."

He frowned as if he couldn't understand why.

"What, you think only doctors and lawyers should be successful?" she asked.

"No, I didn't say that. I admire the fact that you have goals."

"Then you must not like my goal of succeeding in L.A."

"There's nothing wrong with L.A. I just wonder about why you need to go all the way out there. Do you want to rub elbows with the stars, or work at a specific salon, or what? I don't understand."

"I'm not some star stalker. I want to work there be-cause those people are on the cutting edge of style. They make headlines when they walk down a red carpet in a certain designer's clothes, wearing special jewelry, their hair and makeup by the best stylists. If I could be part of that—*when* I'm part of that—everyone will know that I'm successful."

"Everyone as in your family?"

Scarlett frowned, her cappuccino losing its appeal. "Everyone is everyone. Why do you think it's about my family?"

"Because most things are. Me, for example. I'm all about family and friends and town. I know that. It's not exciting or glamorous, but that's what makes me happy."

"You've lost all your ambition?"

"I haven't lost anything by moving back home."

"I can't believe you don't want more. How about being a judge? Don't you want that?"

"I'm doing a favor for a friend and mentor."

She shook her head. "With no ulterior motives? No am-bition to be there permanently?"

"First, who knows what might happen in the future? Second, very few things in life are permanent. Even if I did run for office, I could be voted out in four years. It would be all up to me to make sure I did a good job."

"Just like it will be up to me to succeed in my chosen field. Why can't you understand that?"

"I believe there's a fundamental difference in our reasons, that's all."

"You mean your motives are better than mine."

"I never said that."

"You didn't have to. I understand. You're just like my family. You think I should forget about my dreams because they aren't based on education and conventional careers."

"No! I think you should consider staying around people who care for you rather than trying to win the approval of people you don't even know!"

His outburst made the sudden silence even more shocking. He was being totally mean and unreasonable. What did he know about her industry? What made him an expert on success?

But then, his remark about people who cared sank in, and part of her really wondered what he meant by that.

"Why do you care, James?"

"I care…I…we're friends, right?"

"Oh, right. Friends." Friends with benefits, that's what she'd been thinking. That was before she'd realized how she really felt about James. Correction: how she could potentially feel about him.

He drank his coffee in silence, then said, "It's just…after last night, I assumed you'd considered staying awhile longer. At least through Christmas."

"I haven't."

The words seemed so sharp. So cutting. They had to be said, though.

He flinched just a tiny bit, then visibly firmed his jaw. He took another sip of his cappuccino. "Okay then. My mistake." He looked at his watch. "I guess we'd better get back."

She nodded, but didn't think he was looking at her. Why couldn't she have told him more gently?

"Just one thing."

The last time he'd said that was early this morning, right before he'd kissed her.

"Are you going to wait for your car? Or do you want to go to Weatherford to catch that bus?"

She took a deep breath. "I'm going to wait for my car."

"Good. I think that if you walked away from that car, you'd regret it."

Probably.

"And I don't want to be the reason you walked—or ran—away from something you cared about."

The car, he meant, not the town, the people or him. She felt incredibly alone. "It's not you. It's me."

He nodded, but his expression was way too serious for the James she'd come to know and love—no, admire. She wasn't in love…yet. And if she could leave Brody's Crossing in a week or so, perhaps she'd escape that fate.

AT THE OFFICE the next morning, James poured his energy into replying to the Holmeses' nephew's attorney. The other lawyer had proposed a compromise that would give the nephew a controlling position on the property. *Yeah, good luck with that,* James thought sarcastically. The nephew wasn't getting anything. With a little help from professionals, the Holmeses would be fine. James would see to it.

Then he spent an unproductive five minutes or so thinking about his conversation with Scarlett last night. She'd been so defensive about her profession, so certain everyone was putting her down for the choices she'd made. Maybe he should have told her that he respected her choice of a career, even though he thought she could do almost anything she put her mind to. He hadn't said that, but he'd told her he cared. Wasn't that enough?

Maybe not, if he was still distracted.

Finally, he shook off his unproductive thoughts and wrote up some logs of hours he'd worked for a few clients, and left them for his mother to bill tomorrow or Monday. She probably wouldn't have much to do next week, since he'd be presiding at the spacious Young County courtroom, with its wood benches and paneling, art deco frescoes and tall windows. He liked the big, airy room with the high ceilings and good lighting. It even smelled like a proper courtroom.

The afternoon darkened as five o'clock approached. Finally, James locked his office, went upstairs and suddenly saw Scarlett everywhere. Perched on his sofa, sitting at his dining table. Kissing him. The smell of her would still be on his sheets, in the bed he hadn't bothered to make.

"Damn it," he muttered in the empty, silent space. The only place she hadn't been was his second bedroom, where he had placed his exercise equipment.

That's what he needed—a good workout. He strode down the hall, trying not to think about how he'd felt while carrying Scarlett to his bedroom, and stripped off his business attire. He pulled on athletic pants and a T-shirt, and hit the machines. He had a lot of sweating to do before he eliminated his fixation with Scarlett No-last-name. Hell, he didn't even know her real name!

As he focused on the controlled, repetitive movements of his home gym, he realized that he was just as mad at himself as he was disappointed in Scarlett. She was running away because he'd rushed her into making love. He'd asked her over for a home-cooked meal, knowing where he wanted the evening to end. He'd tried his best to be charming and seductive. She'd made the decision, but it had been his idea. She hadn't come on to him.

She was going to L.A. come hell or high water. If he'd waited, she would have been gone, anyway. They would have never known what could have been.

Now he knew, and he wanted more. He wanted a lot more. Unfortunately, they had barely a week, and he had to be in Graham most of that time, leaving her here in Brody's Crossing with a bunch of new friends and, if all else failed, a bus schedule.

Great. Now what?

SCARLETT CLOSED UP SHOP for Clarissa, who was catching a cold, and Venetia, who'd driven to Graham for Italian food and a movie. The salon fell silent as the last walk-in left and the doors were locked. Scarlett counted the money and checks, filled out a deposit slip and took the zippered bag to the bank's night depository just down the street.

As the bag clunked to the bottom of the vault, she knew a long night stretched in front of her. The café was across the street, right next to James's offices. Over that was his apartment.

The temperature wasn't freezing, but there was a chill in the air, plus the humidity was high, making the cold seep in past her hoodie and sweater, through her jeans. It wasn't a good night to sit in the park, but the café was promising. A sign in the window advertised chicken and dumplings, which sounded great. Her mother sometimes fixed that dish on cold nights. Scarlett suspected she wouldn't be eating "cold weather food" once she got to L.A., and that was kind of sad.

Her knowledge of California cuisine consisted of the avocado and sprouts enhanced club sandwich at the local sub shop. Plus, she'd heard sushi was popular out there. She'd never eaten sushi and the idea of raw fish made her squirm.

So, the café it was. She tucked her hands into the front pocket of her hoodie and crossed the street.

The inside was toasty warm and smelled like heaven. She looked for a booth and saw Raven York wave to her. Raven was sitting with her fiancé, Troy Crawford, so Scarlett went over to say hi.

"I was drawn in by the promise of chicken and dumplings," she said after exchanging greetings.

"We're here to celebrate a little," Raven said. "The house felt a little too confining after the good news that my brother is coming home soon."

"That's great. He's in the military, right?"

"Reserves, serving active duty in Afghanistan."

"I'm glad he's coming home safe and sound."

"He had a slight injury," Raven said, taking Troy's hand. "Some shrapnel hit him near the eye, but his sight wasn't affected. Still, it was a scare."

"I'll bet." Scarlett had seen a news story about all the injuries. The reality felt much closer now.

"Please, join us," Raven said.

"Oh, I don't want to interrupt your celebration dinner."

"Nonsense! It will be nice to have someone to talk to," Raven insisted.

"Please," Troy said. "We'd welcome the opportunity to talk about Cal to someone else. I've worn out all my stories with Raven."

"Okay, then, if you're sure." She settled in the booth opposite the couple.

Within minutes she'd ordered hot tea and milk, then a

bowl of chicken and dumplings with the café's "famous" cornbread on the side. As she listened to Troy talk about his brother, who was the real rancher at the Rocking C, she learned a lot about Texas values. There was a family bond that went way back. They were tied to that land. Troy had scrambled to find a way to save the ranch, but he was worried Cal wouldn't like the changes.

"I guess it's hard to accept something you didn't have a part in deciding," she said. She'd always felt that way. It seemed that everyone else in her family made decisions, and as the youngest, she was supposed to go along.

"The new Rocking C is going to take a lot of acceptance on Cal's part," Troy said, shaking his head. "I just hope that the injury, combined with his war experience, doesn't make it worse."

"I'm sure he'll be glad to get home," Scarlett said, right before her meal was set in front of her. The dish smelled delicious and she couldn't wait to dig in.

A shadow darkened the table. She looked up to see James standing over her. He looked a bit rumpled. His damp hair wasn't tamed and he wore an older—but not ratty— University of Texas sweatshirt and faded jeans. He looked sexy and a little dangerous.

"Hello, Troy. Hi, Raven. Good to see you both." He turned to Scarlett, his eyes intense. "Hi, sweetheart. Didn't we have a date tonight?"

Chapter Ten

"Um, no, not that I remember. I just ordered chicken and dumplings," Scarlett said, which sounded rather silly, after James's dramatic arrival. For someone who was so professional, he could certainly be unpredictable. They hadn't made a date for tonight or any other night. And he had no business calling her "sweetheart".

"No problem." He joined them at the table by sliding in beside Scarlett, literally pushing her over. Their shoulders and hips bumped, and she had to resist the urge to smack his arm as she tried to get settled next to the wall. When the waitress came to the table, he ordered the nightly special also.

The two men chatted about the weather and sports. Raven leaned across the table and talked to Scarlett about the large selection of organic vegetables they'd have at the farmers' market.

Soon everyone's food was on the table. While Raven ate steamed vegetables and a baked potato, Troy seemed to thoroughly enjoy a basket of fried catfish. The "two couples" dynamic felt a little odd, as if both pairs were in equally committed relationships. They weren't. Scarlett didn't want to give her new friends, or anyone watching them from across the restaurant, the idea that she and James were an item.

Despite what he'd claimed in the car last night, openly flaunting her as his "girlfriend" was a mistake. She accepted that he wasn't ashamed of her, but that didn't mean he should tell the world that his idea of a great date was a wild red-haired stylist just passing through his town.

Had he forgotten he was going to be a judge next week? Did he have no sense of self-preservation?

"How are those bison working out?" James asked Troy after they'd taken several bites of their meals.

"Pretty well, except they're a lot stronger and more ornery than cattle. The fences are taking a beating. No one has bred any manners into them."

James chuckled and Scarlett smiled, but there was still tension in the air.

"I wish we didn't have them, since they are being raised for meat, but the Crawfords won't listen to me," Raven said. "At least, I don't think Cal will."

"He won't," Troy stated, reaching for his fries.

They finished their meal with a few interruptions. Friends of Raven and Troy stopped by; clients and friends of James greeted them and chatted. Scarlett felt as though she was truly an outsider, surrounded by these very "settled" people.

Perhaps she should leave as soon as possible….

No, that wasn't fair. She shouldn't make decisions based on a whim, a fleeting sensation. When she was at the salon, she felt at home. Or as "at home" as she could be in this small-town atmosphere.

When she got to Diego's in L.A., she was sure the feeling would be the same, only more exciting. Who knew what celebrities or important people she might see? She could touch the glamour long before she actually had any well-known clients. Wouldn't her family be impressed once she landed some VIP customers?

When she emerged from her daydream, James was laying some bills on the table. He turned to her. "Ready?"

"For what?"

"To talk. To have hot chocolate. I'll use any excuse you'd like to come to my apartment, as long as we get some things straight."

"There's nothing to work out. We're fine."

He took her arm and leaned close so only she could hear. "We're not fine as long as you're avoiding me, acting like I'm barely an acquaintance while we're in public. When you run out on me before I can see you safely back to the salon."

"Walking me 'home' wasn't necessary."

"It would have been the right thing to do."

She rolled her eyes. "Really, James—"

"Really, Scarlett."

She felt as if she should fold her arms over her chest and keep her fanny firmly in the seat. But he probably wouldn't let her do that, at least not without making a scene. "Oh, okay. We'll go to your place, but only to *talk* in private."

"I love it when you're sweet and cooperative."

"Why, James, I didn't know you could be sarcastic."

"I suppose you bring out my hidden traits."

She was pretty sure he didn't consider that a good thing.

The cold wind sent shivers through her, and she walked quickly down the street. James had a tendency to stroll, but tonight she didn't wait for him. Besides, he would probably want to make a statement to anyone who saw them together, and she didn't. She just wanted to be inside, away from wintry weather and curious eyes.

They went up the back stairs and she rubbed her hands together as he retrieved his keys. "The medicinal effects of the chicken and dumplings are fading fast," she complained as he unlocked the door.

"That's because you need a good coat."

"Not in California," she murmured to herself as she sat down on his couch.

"Do you want anything? Hot chocolate, tea or coffee?"

"No, I'm fine. Go ahead with your cross examination, counselor."

"I don't want to question you," he said as he removed his jacket and draped it neatly over the back of a chair. "That's one of the things I don't understand about you. You seem to think that I'm critical. Or maybe you expect people to be critical of you."

Scarlett frowned. "I don't think I do that."

James shrugged. "Think about it. I'm no psychologist so I could be all wrong."

"Yes, you could be," she said, realizing even as she made the statement that she sounded defensive. She looked into her lap where she was twisting the silver band she wore on her thumb. She didn't *expect* people to find fault with her, did she?

She looked up as James sat beside her. "Scarlett, I know you plan to leave here as soon as you can. I wish you wouldn't, but that's your decision. While you're in town, though, I want to spend as much time together as possible. I think you feel the same way."

She nodded, unable to think of a single thing to say that wouldn't sound either flippant or mushy.

"I'm not ashamed of being seen with you. I'm not going to flaunt that we spent the night together, but I'm not ashamed of that, either. Frankly, it's no one's business but ours."

"What if your mother asks?"

He shrugged again. "Then I'd tell her that I like you and plan to spend as much time together as possible."

"Won't she get after you for taking up with—"

"Don't put yourself down again!"

"I'm not!"

He scrubbed his fingers across his forehead and through his hair, leaving choppy, short spikes in front. "Are you being 'Scarlett' when you think people are judging you?"

"What do you mean?"

"I mean that you took a different name and you dyed your hair. I imagine that you took on a new persona. Inside, though, I know you're sweet and caring. You like people or you'd have a different profession." He leaned toward her and took her hands. "Who are you really?"

"What do you mean?"

"I mean, why won't you tell me your real name? Why do you try to keep me from getting any closer to you?"

She pulled her hands away. "There's really no mystery. We both know I'm only here for a few weeks. Why do you need to know my name?"

"It's not that I need to know," he said, running his fingers along her arm, taking her hand in his even as she resisted. "It's that *you* need to tell me."

She shook her head, looking away from his kind, gray eyes. "I'm happy with who I am."

"Oh, sweetheart, I am too. I'd just like… No, I shouldn't say that. Let me just say that if you wanted more, I'd be more than willing."

"I can't want more right now. I already want so much."

He sighed. "I know. L.A. and success."

She looked at their joined hands. "It's my dream."

"I understand. Sometimes, there's room for more than one dream in your life."

"I don't see how that could work."

"I don't know, either. But I have dreams, too." He tipped up her chin. "Dreams of you."

She jumped up from the couch, overwhelmed not by his touch, but by his words. "I need to go. I need to think."

He rose from the couch and stood beside her. "I'll walk you home."

"No! I need to be alone."

"I understand. I'll walk you to the salon and leave you alone. I promise." He reached down and rubbed her arms, smiling in a sad way, as if he knew how confused she was. "Although, I'd love for you to stay with me."

She nodded, hugging her arms around herself. "I've got a phone call to make."

James grabbed his jacket and slipped it on. "If you need me, you can call me, too."

"I know." And she did. James was super dependable. One of her top priorities, for as long as she could remember, was learning to depend on herself, not someone else. That was part of the "be true to herself" philosophy she'd adopted when she'd realized she was different than her brother and sister.

And a disappointment to her parents.

At the back door of the salon, James shielded her from the wind with his body. In the illumination from the security lights mounted high above, she looked into James's eyes and felt a combination of excitement and dread, a fluttery feeling in her stomach and a tightness in her heart.

It would be way too easy to let herself fall for him. And then she'd be here in Texas, going nowhere in her career. Or in the life she had planned for herself.

James kissed her with tenderness and passion. She

leaned into him, kissing him back, giddy with the promise of passion that would be unfulfilled, at least for now.

"If you change your mind, call me or come back to my apartment."

She nodded, then unlocked the door and went inside. She could see him in her mind's eyes, waiting on the back porch until she'd locked the deadbolt.

Her smile faded, though, when she remembered what she needed to do. She hadn't called home in several days, and then just to let her parents know she'd had some "minor car trouble" that had delayed her trip.

Settling on the sofa, she scrolled through her cell phone address book until she found "Folks." As the phone rang, she imagined what they might be doing. Her dad was probably watching TV while her mother wrapped Christmas presents.

"Hi, Mom. What's up?"

They chatted for a minute or so about how her parents were getting ready for the holidays. They were putting up a smaller tree this year, for one thing, and giving gift certificates instead of presents, for another.

"Gosh, I've only been gone a couple of weeks, and already you're downsizing."

"Just a little," her mother admitted. "It's just not the same now that we're empty nesters. Of course, that will change when your niece or nephew is born."

"I guess I really will be an aunt." Aunt Scarlett. She liked the sound of that.

"I hope you can come back when the baby is born."

"I'm not sure." She didn't know if she'd have the money to fly home or the ability to take off days from work.

"Um, Mom, you know I really like what I'm doing. Styling hair. I'm good at it, too."

"Yes, I know." She could *almost* hear her mother sigh.

"I know you and Dad aren't thrilled with my choice, so I was just wondering…if I wasn't a stylist, what would you have wanted me to be?"

Her mother paused as if considering the question, then said, "I'm not sure. I mean, you don't like math and you didn't enjoy studying that much."

"I didn't enjoy studying old facts and dates and things that don't apply to real life." She'd been fine at cosmetology school at learning techniques, formulas and regulations.

"Well, yes. But when you get an education, you have to take some classes that don't immediately apply to what you want to do."

"I have an education," Scarlett defended.

This time she heard her mother sigh. "I meant a college education."

"I know what you mean. So, you never did answer my question. What would you and Dad have preferred that I become? I know you're not happy that I'm a stylist."

"We're not unhappy. We just think you could be so much more."

"Like what?"

"Well, perhaps, if you'd wanted to, you could have been an attorney or a teacher."

"Believe me, Mom, I would have made a terrible attorney." After seeing how conservative and…and stuffy James was, she couldn't imagine leading that kind of life. And, heaven forbid, she couldn't be in any kind of business or corporate setting.

"A teacher, then. You like children."

"I suppose. I had a little girl in last week, as a matter of fact." She told her mother about Hailey, ready to divert this conversation to what was actually going on in her life, not what someone else wanted from her.

Scarlet realized her mother hadn't said anything for a few moments. Then she heard a sniff. Was her mother crying?

"Honey, that is so sweet. I never thought about all the ways your job might affect people. But no matter how important your career is to you, please think about coming back for the birth of our first grandchild."

"I'll do what I can. I'd better go now, Mom."

After Scarlett disconnected and placed her phone back in the pocket of her hoodie, she slumped on the couch. Only the lamp on the countertop across the room kept her company. Loneliness pressed around her.

At the restaurant, she'd felt alone with Raven and Troy. Even after James came in and sat with her, she hadn't felt as if they were a couple. As if she belonged. Talking to James had made her want to call her mother, but that, despite her mother's praise, had only made her feel more isolated from the family.

Maybe there was something in the way she made decisions that made her different. She didn't *want* to feel isolated, did she? She didn't think so. She enjoyed the feeling of belonging in a salon. She made friends with her coworkers. She enjoyed meeting new people.

So, what made her feel so alone? Had she really pushed James away with flippant remarks? Maybe. But part of her personality was being cheerful. Her friends had called her spunky. That was true; she had spunk or she wouldn't be moving across the country alone.

She sat for a while longer, the silence and darkness pressing closer and closer until she jumped up from the couch. Perhaps this was a good time to be honest with James, at least about her feelings at the moment.

Within a few minutes she climbed the metal stairs and

stood at the back door of James's apartment. When he answered her knock, she stepped into his arms.

"I want to spend the night with you," she said against his warm chest. "I want to be with you." *For now.*

She felt him smile against her hair as he held her close. Then he pulled her inside and closed the door.

"GOOD MORNING."

Scarlett's head shot up. "What time is it?"

"Not even six o'clock yet," he replied. "It's still dark outside."

She relaxed back to the pillow. "Oh, good."

"I think you should move in with me until it's time for you to leave. This is a much better mattress than that sofa bed back at the salon."

"True," she murmured, closing her eyes. "But what will the neighbors say?"

"The men will be jealous. The women will—"

"Be jealous, too," she said.

He smiled. "I'm not so sure about that. I'm not exactly a sex symbol around town."

"That's only because they haven't slept with you." Scarlett moved closer as he stroked her cheek. She frowned. "Or, at least I assume most of them haven't graced your bed or the back seat of your car."

"None that are currently living here," he said. "I can't say that I was a perfect saint in high school, but the girls in question graduated and moved away."

"How about Jennifer Wright?"

She'd been Jennifer Hopkins when they dated. "Girlfriend, not lover."

"Oh. Good. Her daughter, Hailey, is very sweet, and it

just blows the whole family image to think about you and Jennifer together."

"So, anyway," he said, getting back to his point and away from the issue of old girlfriends, "my bed is much more comfortable. Stay with me."

"I'll think about it."

"Oh, and one more thing. My parents are going to Wichita Falls to visit friends and do some Christmas shopping. I'll be at the house for the weekend. Come stay with me there."

"I need to work on Saturday."

"Then come after you get finished for the day. I'll cook you a meal, and I promise you won't have to sleep on the lumpy couch."

"No?"

"No. You'll be snug as can be."

"With you."

"Upstairs, under the eaves." He kissed her cheek. "Old farmhouse. Very quaint." He pulled the comforter down and kissed her shoulder. "Lots of quilts." His hand crept lower and cupped her breast. "If that's not enough, there's always heated massage oil."

Scarlett giggled and pulled the covers up. "Okay! I'll come out to the ranch with you."

"I'll be in Graham most of the day today, getting ready for Monday."

"Okay, Judge James. Maybe you could get a TV show."

"Doubtful, since I'm only a judge for a week."

"Yes, but you might be one when you grow up."

He playfully swatted her bottom. "Don't be snarky. You're younger than me."

"Yes, but I know what I want to be."

"Yeah, I know." And she was going after it in California, but he didn't voice that depressing thought. She was here now, and he planned to take advantage of their relationship for as long as possible.

"Will you have dinner with me tonight?"

"Sure. As I said before, you're a great diversion, and my options are limited."

He ignored her flippant remarks. He knew he was more than a diversion, even if she didn't want to admit it. "I wish I could take you out to a really nice dinner at a fancy restaurant, but we'll have to settle for Dewey's."

"That's fine. I don't have the wardrobe with me for fancy restaurants."

Sometime later, as he cleaned up the kitchen after breakfast, she came out of the bathroom looking young and fresh without any makeup. Even her hair appeared softer, with curls instead of spikes.

"We'll have a good time this weekend. I'm looking forward to you seeing the ranch."

"Me, too. I like animals. Did I tell you that?"

"No, but I'm not surprised."

Later, as he drove to Graham, he thought about the coming weekend. He didn't really have any massage oil, but he'd get some. Yes, he rather liked the idea. He'd have to make sure he and Scarlett didn't slide out of his double bed, though. And he'd have to remember to wash his own sheets, rather than leaving them for his mother to find.

He felt like a kid again. Or at least a horny teenager.

This weekend, instead of simply feeding the few cattle, the two old horses, the three dogs, the small flock of chickens, the miscellaneous ducks and birds, he'd have a new activity: making love in his old bedroom. Something he'd always wanted to do.

When he was married, Babs had never wanted to stay

at the house with his parents. He'd been irritated at the time, but now he was glad. He wouldn't have any old memories to erase before making new ones with Scarlett.

Not that she could ever be confused with anyone else.

Chapter Eleven

James went to Graham for a final meeting with Judge Bell and staff at the county offices before assuming his position on Monday. There weren't many cases scheduled for the week, but two attorneys were fighting over evidence in a conspiracy to commit fraud case, and they could file motions that had to be heard. The fraud involved a significant inheritance, a bogus relative and a phony corporation.

"Let's get lunch," Harve Bennett, the district attorney, suggested as the morning meeting wound down. "How about the tearoom across the street? We can walk there and get back here fairly quickly, so we can be finished before the sun sets."

That was fine with James, since all he thought about outside the judicial system was meeting Scarlett for dinner and taking her back to his place.

As the group of men walked past the Confederate memorial, a determined-looking older man marched up to them. "I want to talk to you," he said gruffly.

"Since when do we have to bring in outsiders?" he asked Judge Bell. "Especially ones still wet behind the ears?"

"Milton Bastine, I don't think you've met James Brody in person," Bell said.

James extended his hand, but the older man ignored him. "I don't need to meet him to know what's going on."

"Nothing is 'going on,'" the judge said.

"You're still upset that I ran against you last year," Bastine declared. "That's why you brought in an out-of-towner."

"This is the Young County court, not the Graham court. I think you'd be wise to remember that, Milt."

"This is the county seat. Besides, I have forty years more experience than this pup," Bastine said, pointing at James with his thumb.

"Watch it," Judge Bell warned. "You're talking about a soon-to-be sitting judge."

"Oh, you don't scare me. Either one of you. You'll regret not choosing experience over his pretty-boy looks."

"Mr. Bastine, if you have an issue with my qualifications," James said, "perhaps we should talk about it privately. I don't think the public sidewalk is the right place for what appears to be a jealous confrontation."

The judge smiled, but Bastine became even more furious. "You'll regret mocking me."

"I don't think so," James replied coolly. "Hopefully, I won't see you before me in court."

Bastine turned an alarming shade of purple, spun on his heel and stalked back to his car.

"That man has some anger issues," James said.

"You're right. He's jealous," the judge agreed.

"He's a bunch of hot air," another lawyer added.

"Don't let him worry you," the district attorney advised. "He barely has any clients, and none of them will be before the bench next week. I'll see to that."

They watched Bastine peel out of the parking area, way too fast for safety, especially considering his age and probable lack of reflexes. But that was a job for the police, not the legal teams, so they continued on to their lunch with no more incidents.

By the time James finished his meetings for the day and stopped by the drugstore, he was more than ready to see Scarlett.

THEY ATE DINNER Friday night at Dewey's, then went back to James's apartment to sleep in his comfortable bed. Not that they went to sleep right away, Scarlett remembered the next morning. He'd rubbed her tired feet, massaging away her stress. Then he'd worked his way up her legs, creating an entirely different kind of tension.

As she prepared for work on Saturday morning, she knew she was looking forward to the weekend—and to spending that time with James—much more than she should. To get herself grounded, she used her cell phone to call Diego, just to check in. She didn't think anything could have happened to change her status as a new intern arriving in January, but she should make certain.

Sure enough, he was looking forward to her arrival. He commiserated about the car trouble, but didn't offer to help. Not that she'd expected him to. She wasn't his employee yet, and car trouble went beyond employer-employee relationships, anyway.

Hopefully, she'd make friends with her fellow stylists at the salon. She'd be the "new girl," but she was intent on fitting in quickly.

After all, hadn't she slipped right into the situation here at Clarissa's House of Style? If she could fit in here, she could fit in anywhere!

As she dropped her cell phone into her pocket and adjusted her Santa hat so it flopped just right, Clarissa and Venetia came in, bringing with them cool air and a hint of evergreen.

"Good morning!" Clarissa bustled forward, taking off her coat and gloves. "I swear, it's a real treat to come in to fresh brewed coffee, the lights and heat already on," she said, giving Scarlett a big smile.

"We brought you a Danish," Venetia said. "They were really good this morning at the café."

"Thanks." Scarlett took the bag and peeked inside. Cherry, her favorite. How thoughtful. Now Venetia was practically an old friend. And Clarissa acted more like a benevolent aunt than an employer, much different than Diego. Not that she could really compare the two vastly different lifestyles and situations.

"We're going to have our annual Christmas lunch with the girls at the café next Wednesday at noon," Clarissa said as she filled a mug with coffee and added half-and-half from the refrigerator. "We want you to come, of course, but don't feel as if you need to bring a gift. We have this long-standing gift exchange, but everyone knows you haven't had a car or anything to go shopping."

"Oh, I shouldn't intrude on your lunch."

"No, we want you to come. Just bring yourself, that's what we say. We'll have fun. Bobbi Jean always makes dessert for us and everyone in the café."

"If I'm here," Scarlett hedged. "I haven't heard from Claude on how long it's taking to put in the new engine." The idea of driving away from Brody's Crossing made her panic, much as the idea of pink smocks made her feel trapped. Why couldn't she pick one emotion and stick to it?

"I hope you're still here," Venetia said. "We'll be busy next week, and we could really use an extra set of hands."

Scarlett's ten o'clock came through the door then, and everyone got to work. She barely had time to think of her upcoming weekend, much less next week, as she snipped and styled and colored her way to closing time.

"THIS IS REALLY NEAT," Scarlett said as she walked beside James back to the house. "I haven't been around so many animals before."

"My parents just keep the ones they can't part with, plus some beef cattle. Back when they were younger, before my dad's stroke, they kept a whole herd of Santa Gertrudis and a half-dozen cutting horses."

"Was if hard for them to give it up?"

James nodded. "My dad fought it for a while. He thought he'd be back one hundred percent, and things would go back to the way there were. But over time, he realized that he was getting a little older and he wasn't going to be working cattle anymore."

"Is he very affected by the stroke?"

"No, he's really not. He still has some weakness on his left side, but it's not very noticeable. He did his physical therapy. My mother worked with him, and we had lots of volunteers who came out here to help. When my mother was tired, there was always someone else who could pitch in. That's one reason I love this town so much."

"I can see that. I'm sure your parents are respected and well liked. That's why everyone is so helpful."

"Yes, they've been a part of the community for a long time. Church, my school, town projects. They always participated. They never said it, but I think they felt a special responsibility because of our connection to the founding of Brody's Crossing."

"Sounds idyllic. My neighborhood was nice, but not that close. Most people worked long hours, and went their own ways. We'd drive into the garage, shut the door and be in our own homes or yards most of the time."

"Sounds kind of unfriendly."

"I guess it does to you, based on how close you are to friends and neighbors. But that's the way I grew up. That's my reality."

"So you're going to work in a new place where you won't know anyone, and you'll probably live in an apartment building full of strangers. That really seems cold."

"I'll get used to it," she said, but wondered if she would feel lonely. Would the excitement of the salon make up for the loneliness?

Yes, of course it would. How many people got the type of opportunity she was getting at Diego's? A high school counselor had told her that she had an obligation to herself to go after what she wanted in life.

She wanted to be a stylist to the stars. She had for as long as she could remember, as soon as she realized she wanted to do hair. She'd always been great at duplicating the styles of her favorite celebrities on her friends and family.

Unfortunately, her mother got stuck on the 1980s Linda Gray bob-with-bangs style. No matter how many times Scarlett offered to update her look, she declined. The only progress Scarlett had made was to get all the shoulder pads out of her mom's dresses, blouses and jackets.

"So," she said as they returned to the house, "what are you fixing for supper?"

"I thought I'd make you my special baby back ribs."

"Yum. Let's get started."

She worked side by side with James in the kitchen. He'd obviously gone to the grocery earlier today. He'd marinated the slabs of ribs and gotten all the fixings for salad and loaded baked potatoes. The Brodys had a nice gas grill that James said got lots of use from his dad.

By the time they'd finished grilling, the sun had long since set and the temperature had dropped to near freezing. James herded the dogs inside for the night, shut down the grill and treated Scarlett as if she was an honored guest rather than a temporary lover.

He built a fire in the cozy family room and they settled in to watch the flames and listen to the logs pop. Two of the dogs curled up on the rug as Scarlett tucked her feet beneath a hand-knit afghan on the couch. "I'm so full," she said. "You are a terrific cook."

"I'm limited as to what I cook or grill, but I know what I like. I'm glad you enjoyed dinner."

"I really, really did," she said, laying her head on his shoulder. She felt warm, full and happy. James smelled of barbecue smoke and subtle cologne. She closed her eyes and inhaled, enjoying the moment. Enjoying the man and his family home. She told herself she should thank him for asking her to join him this weekend, but she was so sleepy. She'd close her eyes for just a minute….

JAMES WATCHED THE PLAY of firelight on Scarlett's relaxed features. Her red hair seemed to turn to dark, mysterious flames. She appeared young and almost girlish tonight, snuggled next to him on the sofa's soft pillows.

He sighed and frowned, feeling alone in the dark, quiet house. Would he feel this way when Scarlett was gone to California? Or would his mood be even worse?

She seemed so right, next to him on the couch. Sleeping beside him in bed. Laughing at a joke they shared, or entertaining him with witty comments.

He didn't miss being married, but he missed *this*. A

comfortable evening at home. A warm fire and even warmer woman. A good meal and a couple of dogs curled at his feet. What could be better? He'd never had all of this at once—a wife but no dogs, a fireplace but a chilly woman, a good meal but a one-bedroom apartment.

Maybe it was time to think about having it all.

As if she could read his thoughts, Scarlett moaned in her sleep and snuggled next to him. He tightened his arm, leaned down and kissed her head. He vaguely recalled a conversation where someone had accused him of being rich. He wasn't. He made enough for himself to live comfortably and pay his bills, but he wasn't rolling in dough. He couldn't, for example, buy the office building where he worked and lived, even though that might be a good option in the near future. If he had a child, he'd have to make compromises to create a college fund. His clients paid him promptly, perhaps because he didn't charge nearly as much as a big city lawyer.

He wouldn't move, though. He loved this town and felt tied to the people and the land. When he'd gone to school and moved away to live, he'd lost the connection, and he'd subconsciously missed the places and people. Now he felt grounded, even though he wasn't rich.

Perhaps he should consider running for office. He could set his sights on one of the county positions, earn his salary there for several years, and use his experience and name identification to boost his law practice. Plus, he'd get a nice retirement package as a judge. It was an option he should consider if he was thinking about a family and a future.

Scarlett's hand fell to his lap, bringing him back to the present. Would she care what he did? Would she stay? He wasn't sure there was any condition that would keep her in Texas. She was hell-bent on getting to Diego in California. She'd practically laughed at the idea of working in a place like Clarissa's House of Style.

Would she laugh at the idea of being married to a lawyer? A judge? Probably. She viewed herself as a free spirit, an independent and self-styled individual.

She needed family, though, even if she thought they didn't appreciate her. Scarlett didn't realize how defined she was by the values and traditions of her parents. Even if she didn't agree with them, she reacted to them. She didn't want to give up that car, she wanted to remember the Christmas traditions, and she wore fashions that would make her folks respond, either positively or negatively.

"Scarlett, what am I going to do with you?" he whispered against her hair. But she might take that option away by leaving as soon as the engine was installed.

The thought was enough to make him consider sabotaging the Benz. Consider, not do. Not if he seriously wanted to be a judge or other elected official.

"What time is it?" she murmured.

"I don't know. You haven't been sleeping that long," he answered.

"Oh. I didn't know where I was for a moment."

"You're with me, at the ranch." He tipped her chin up and smiled into her sleepy eyes. "You do remember me, don't you?"

Her smile lit up her face. Her skin appeared golden and warm in the firelight, and he wanted to strip her naked and kiss her all over. "I remember you," she said. "You're that preppy lawyer who gives me a hard time."

"Um-hmm. I'll show you a hard time," he said, pushing her back into the pillows. He kissed her smiling mouth as he pulled her beneath him.

Her lips parted and she kissed him back, as hungry for

him as she'd been for the meal earlier. She held him tightly as they sank deeper into the sofa. Even though they'd made love almost ten times already, *this* felt new and exciting.

He tugged at her sweater, then moved lower to tease that tempting belly button ring. He lingered to unfasten her jeans and run his tongue along the edge of her lacy panties while she writhed beneath him. When she grabbed his hair and pulled, though, he decided to temporarily leave his quest.

She kissed him again and pulled at his clothes. If he didn't slow them down, they'd be naked in less than a minute. "We have to go upstairs," he rasped.

"Why? I like it here."

"No condoms."

She dropped her head to the pillows. "Damn."

"Besides, I have a particular fantasy that involves you in my teenage bedroom," he said between nips to her neck.

"Do I get to be naked?"

"Absolutely. And multiorgasmic."

"Oh, that's a big word for a teenager."

"I'm a big boy now," he growled into her neck.

Scarlett laughed, pulling him close. "You certainly are. Lead the way."

"I'll do better than that." He eased off her warm body, stood beside the couch, scooped her into his arms and took the stairs to his old room two at a time.

Chapter Twelve

The next morning Scarlett woke with a smile on her face and not a speck of clothing on her body. She'd snuggled against James in his double bed under the eaves all night. She hated to move from beneath the thick comforter, away from his warmth, but nature called. Besides, she owed him breakfast. He'd cooked dinner for her several times.

She kissed his cheek, making him groan and smile in his sleep. She slipped out of bed and headed to the bathroom across the hall. Darn it. She was naked and her overnight bag was on the floor in the living room. Oh, well. She'd borrow something of James's. Within ten minutes she'd showered, and shortly after that, she was dressed in a large BCHS sweatshirt, rolled-up athletic pants and his oversize socks. She grinned and headed downstairs.

Life was strange. Here she was on a Texas ranch, enjoying a calm weekend with a preppy lawyer who kissed like a dream and made her toes curl. She stirred the eggs in his mother's skillet and sprinkled cheddar cheese she'd found in the refrigerator.

"Something smells good," James said, walking into the kitchen. He wore jeans, a cable-knit cotton sweater and thick socks. He looked like a Ralph Lauren ad as he strolled over and kissed her temple. "Nice fashion statement."

"I was desperate. It was this or my birthday suit."

"I didn't get a vote on that option."

"No, you didn't," she said, leaning back and kissing him. "Now, don't distract me."

"What are you making?"

"Just a simple breakfast. The bacon is in the oven, staying warm. I'll make toast—"

"I'll make it," he offered.

Together they finished putting together the meal. The round table was in a nook with a bay window that overlooked the patio and pasture beyond the picket fence. "It's really homey here," Scarlett said as she sipped coffee.

"I'm lucky. I have good parents and I had an unremarkable childhood, except for a few pranks."

"Pranks?" She vaguely remembered him mentioning his childhood transgressions. "What kind of pranks?"

He shrugged. "Normal stuff. Nothing you'd be interested in."

"Oh, I'll be the judge of that. Come on. You're too perfect. Tell me something naughty you did."

James waggled his eyebrow and grinned. "I made out with Mary Rogers in the girls restroom at the high school field house during cheerleading tryouts."

"No, I want something…big. Something you might have been arrested for."

"Why would you assume I did anything that bad?"

She took a bite of eggs. "Just hoping."

He smiled. "Okay, here's something. When I was seventeen, Wyatt McCall and I got hold of a parasail. We rigged it up behind Wyatt's pickup truck and took turns pulling each other on this little road near Newcastle." James laughed and shook his head. "That was fun…and really stupid. We could have killed ourselves."

"Wow, that was reckless. Did your parents find out?"

"No, we weren't caught, but they overheard us talking about it at our graduation party, and boy, were they mad."

"A little late to ground you, I suppose."

"Yes, but I got grounded for other things."

"Such as?"

He sighed. "Well, when I was in ninth grade, a group of us streaked past a wedding."

"What do you mean?"

"My friend's older sister, whom he didn't really like very much, was getting married at the church downtown. The one across from the feed store, near McCaskie's garage. Anyway, we stripped off our clothes, waited for the wedding party to come down the steps, and ran naked past them, around the corner of the church, while everyone else was throwing rice."

"Oh, no! That was terrible of you."

"I know, but at the time, it seemed totally justified, based on my friend's assertions that his sister had made his life hell."

Scarlett folded her arms on the table and leaned toward James. "This is great stuff. Tell me more."

He chuckled, seemingly in touch with the spirit of confession. "Once, we dyed our hair the school colors for the homecoming game. Wyatt was the quarterback and I was a wide receiver. Actually, the whole team dyed their hair."

"What are your team colors?"

He pointed toward the purple letters outlined in bright yellow on the gray sweatshirt she wore. "Purple and yellow."

"Now I don't feel nearly as weird having bright red hair."

He laughed again, and Scarlett felt so relaxed. If only

life could be like this, it would be worth living in a small town. Her smiled faded, and she looked away. Life didn't stay the same, though. James would go back to his apartment on Sunday night, she'd go back to the salon Monday morning. And she couldn't forget about his temporary judgeship next week.

Or her upcoming exodus to California.

"So whatever happened to your friend Wyatt?"

"He went to Stanford, bought out some computer company and became rich enough to do whatever he wants."

"Wow. That's a big change from getting in trouble in a small town."

"I suppose, but we sure had a lot of fun."

"I'll clean up the dishes," James offered. "Then we can go to the barn and feed the animals."

"Okay. Good idea."

Within a few minutes, she and James were trudging out to the barn. While he measured feed into buckets, she explored the stalls and talked to the goats and horses. The cattle were out in the pasture.

She poked her head into what James called "the hay room," which was really an empty stall stacked with rectangular bales of hay. The floor of the stall was covered in deep, loose hay and smelled so fragrant. She wanted to lie down and make hay angels!

And then she got another idea, one that wasn't nearly as angelic. Within moments, while James finished feeding, she made a big mound of hay, stripped off his old sweatshirt and pants, pulled off her socks and kicked off her shoes.

"Scarlett, where are you?" he called.

"Back here in the hay room," she said, lying back on the pile. It wasn't nearly as comfortable as she'd imagined. The dried grass poked her in places she didn't want to be poked, and felt way too itchy to be sexy.

She was wiggling around, scratching her back, when James walked into the stall. "Wow!" he said succinctly, reaching for the snap on his jeans.

"Wait! It's really itchy down here."

He grabbed her discarded clothes and pulled her to her feet, kissing her along the way. Then he spread the sweatshirt and his sweater on the hay and, with an evil glint in his eyes, tossed her down. "Better?"

She wriggled a little to get comfortable. "Yeah," she said, crooking her finger toward him.

He grinned and lowered himself on her. "This was a fantasy I hadn't even considered. Nice thinking."

"I aim to please."

"You certainly do," he murmured before kissing her deeply. In the background, she heard the sounds of the animals moving, munching their feed. The rest of the world seemed far away as James ran his hands over her body, as his kisses became more demanding.

"Hello! James, are you in here?"

Scarlett felt him pause, then stiffen. "Oh, no." He leaped to his feet, immediately grabbing his jeans.

Just hide, Scarlett mouthed, scooting off the sweater, sweatshirt and mound of hay.

He shook his head, yanked on his jeans and fastened them. Unfortunately, the sound of the zipper seemed to echo loudly in the barn.

He shut his eyes, pulled Scarlett close and whispered in her ear, "Demanding Desmond."

"James Brody, what's going on in there?"

He looked up, just enough to see over the solid wall of the stall. "Oh, I'm just taking care of the ranch while my parents are in Wichita Falls." He motioned for Scarlett to stay down, which she gladly did as she searched for the pants she'd been wearing.

"We brought your mother a red velvet cake from the church Christmas bazaar. Myra Hammer said Carolyn might not be feeling well."

"No, she's fine," James answered. Scarlett listened to their voices grow closer, and resisted the urge to moan. Where were those pants? She had to learn to be neater when she stripped off her clothes.

"I'll be out in a minute, ladies. Why don't you wait for me at the house?"

"Oh, we don't mind the barn, do we, Joan?"

Joan?

"No, not at all," another voice answered.

James looked back at Scarlett and shrugged. Apparently he didn't know this person, either. He leaned down and pulled his sweater on over his head.

Scarlett found the pants in the corner, beneath a pile of hay. Now, where was the sweatshirt? She'd just had it!

"James, there's someone I want you to meet," Mrs. Desmond said.

He popped back up. "Yes?"

"This is my friend Joan Lindell from Loving." Mrs. Desmond paused a moment. "Joan, this is James Brody, the attorney who's going to be filling in for the judge in Graham."

"Oh, *he's* the one," Joan said, as if James were personally repulsive to her, which was a very odd reaction.

Scarlett started to pull on the pants, but just as she stuck her leg in, the most horrible, hairy spider crawled right up the fabric, going for her.

"Yikes!" she yelled, and threw the pants as hard as she

could. Her heart raced and she felt as if a hundred of those horrid things were crawling on her.

Unfortunately, she discovered when she looked up, she'd thrown the pants right over the wall of the stall. James's wide eyes followed their path.

"What in the world?"

Scarlett hurried over to James, hunkering down so she'd be shielded by the wall in case someone looked over the top and noticed a naked, redheaded woman.

She probably couldn't pass herself off as a goat or a horse. And sure enough, that nosy ol' biddy looked right over the top of the stall to see what was going on. As if it was any of her business.

James closed his eyes, sighed and pulled Scarlett close. "I really think you should wait for me at the house."

"What in the world!" Ashley Desmond's mother leaned over and looked Scarlett in the eyes as she straightened. She could barely see over the top of the five-foot-something-inch high stall. Mrs. Desmond probably couldn't see much more than hay-infused red hair and guilty green eyes.

"You!"

"I guess I don't disguise well."

"We had no idea we'd be interrupting you and your *friend,*" Mrs. Desmond sniped.

James shrugged. "I did suggest you wait for me at the house."

Scarlett could practically hear Mrs. Desmond purse her thin lips. "Do your parents have any idea that you have company out here while they're gone?"

"Mrs. Desmond, I hardly think that's any of your business. Now, thanks for the cake. I really have to go. It's kind of chilly out here, don't you think?"

When the ladies had marched away, James turned to Scarlett. "Well, that was a perfectly awful end to a wonderful morning," he said.

AFTER THE CHURCH LADIES left, Scarlett's mood was subdued. James accepted her excuse that she had some laundry to do at the salon, and drove her back to town. Or maybe she didn't want his parents to know she'd been at the ranch this weekend. He kissed her goodbye, then returned to clean up after himself and Scarlett before his folks arrived.

He hadn't planned to keep it a secret from them, although it wasn't Delores Desmond's business. She'd taken a particular interest in his personal life, especially explaining who he was to Joan Lindell. Why? He had no idea, except that some people were just meddling biddies.

After he stripped the sheets from his old bed, he washed them with the bath towels and finished cleaning up the kitchen. The afternoon dragged on as he fed the animals and threw the ball for the dogs, once the day warmed up a little. Just when he was thinking that he'd go on back to town, his parents drove up in his dad's extended cab pickup.

Despite the earlier unwelcome visit, James's mood lifted upon seeing his parents. They appeared happy and rested.

"We had a great time," his mother said as his dad unloaded bags from the back seat of the vehicle. James had been warned not to look.

"I'm glad. There weren't any problems here. Delores Desmond and a friend of hers brought a red velvet cake from your Sunday school class. Apparently they were concerned about you since you weren't at church."

"Oh, that was nice." She peered at the white frosted

cake. "Apparently red dye and chocolate is a new cure for whatever ails you."

"I suppose. Just so you know, when the ladies came out, Scarlett was here. They might mention it, given their penchant for gossip. Also, the other woman, Joan Lindell, seemed curious about me serving as a judge next week in Graham. I'm not sure what that's all about."

"I have no idea, but I'll find out."

"It's probably nothing," he said.

"So," his mother said slowly, and he knew what was coming, "you and Scarlett. You've been quite the item lately."

"I like her. A lot." He shrugged. "It's not serious, though, Mom. She's leaving for California. She's made that clear."

"I wasn't sure about her at first, but I like her now. She's a very caring person."

"Yes, she is, but she's hell-bent on going to L.A."

His mother sighed. "Well, I wish she'd stay. Clarissa is so happy to have her there, and she needs an extra stylist. Of course, I kind of wish Scarlett would tell us her real name. Do you know it?"

"No, I don't. I haven't asked, and she didn't volunteer." And yes, not knowing bothered him.

His mother nodded. "And her hair! Well, I'd like to see her as a brunette or a blonde, maybe. Or even a more natural shade of red. I don't understand why she wants it so bright."

"She's making a statement, kind of like a tattoo."

"Well, I don't understand those, either."

Then he definitely shouldn't tell his mother about the little symbol of Georgia he'd discovered low on Scarlett's read end. His new nickname for her should be "peach cheeks," he thought with a grin.

"You're grinning," his mother said.

"Sorry."

She shook her head. "Would you like to take some red velvet cake home with you? For you and Scarlett, maybe? Your father and I can't eat all this."

He was pretty sure what Scarlett's reaction would be to a piece of that particular cake. "No, thanks, Mom. I don't think we could eat a bite of it."

He packed up his clothes and toiletries, then visited with his dad while they watched the last quarter of a Cowboys game. Finally, as the sun began to set, he headed back to Brody's Crossing. He needed to swing by the salon, see what Scarlett was up to, and discover whether she was staying at his place tonight.

He'd missed his comfortable king-size bed last night, although he had to admit the double mattress beneath the eaves had been cozy and warm because she was with him.

SCARLETT SLIPPED OUT OF James's bed extra early on Monday morning, long before sunrise. She wanted to be well away from him before he left for his judicial duties, all dressed in the suit and tie he'd taken out of his closet the night before. Beyond preppy to professional chic. On Sunday night she'd trimmed his hair back to a sedate side part, just like he'd worn before she'd come to town. He looked successful and imposing, not at all small-town and not at all like her playful lover.

His alarm rang as she was putting on her shoes. She sat down on the side of the bed. "Wake up, sleepyhead. Time to be old, sedate and stodgy."

"Never," he said, twisting the pillow around and slowly opening his eyes. "You're dressed."

"I need to get going. You have a lot to do today."

"I thought we could share breakfast. And I was going to walk you back to the salon. It's still dark outside."

"No, I'll be fine. There's no reason for you to get dressed right now. I need to head out. I have a busy day too."

He sat up, suddenly all serious and intense. "You're not doing anything…weird, are you? You're not going anywhere today, for example?"

"No, Your Honor," she said, raising her right hand. "I swear."

He seemed to relax. "Okay, then. Would you like to have dinner tonight at Dewey's?"

"Sure. About six-thirty?"

"Sounds good. I'll pick you up, unless you want to meet me here." He reached for her hands. "You could help me change clothes. Wash all that judicial atmosphere off my back."

"No, thanks. I'll be hungry. I'll wash your back later."

"Okay, then." He leaned forward and kissed her temple, then the side of her neck. "I'll miss you during the day."

"Hopefully, I won't do anything to get hauled in front of the court."

"I'm sure you won't. I think everyone has decided not to sue you for anything. I'll see you tonight, peach cheeks."

Scarlett smiled at the new nickname and let herself out the side door, then down the metal stairs to the small garden below. She turned and headed back to the salon, pulling her hoodie tight around her and trying to imagine her day, stretching long in front of her, while James was busy in court down in Graham.

Somehow, now that he was serving as a judge, their differences seemed all that more pronounced. She'd forgotten them for a while this weekend, out at his parents' ranch, until the church ladies came with their snippy comments and red velvet cake.

But they'd reminded her that she was only a liability for

James Brody, upstanding lawyer and former prankster. He'd moved on with his life, while she was just getting started with hers. In California.

One of the things she needed to do today was check with Claude to see when her car would finally be ready. She couldn't put off leaving much longer.

JAMES ARRIVED EARLY at the courthouse, since he hadn't taken time for breakfast with Scarlett. She'd seemed distracted, but trying to put on a good show of support. She was so darn sensitive to his reputation and community standing. Of course, Demanding Desmond and her sidekick, Joan Lindell, could upset anyone.

It wasn't easy pushing aside thoughts of Scarlett. The vision of her driving off in that aging Mercedes kept flashing in his mind.

The image of him chasing after her, calling her name, seemed equally real.

He sighed and settled back in the judge's leather chair. There was nothing on the docket this morning. He was supposed to be concentrating on a memo from the district attorney that had been added to the fraud file. James's mind, however, continued to be on Scarlett. He sure wished he could be certain she hadn't been doing anything rash— such as leaving while he was out of town.

The clerk of the court knocked, interrupting his thoughts. With a silent thanks for the diversion, he sat up straight and tuned all his attention to answering a procedural question about potential evidence displays.

At lunchtime he, D.A. Harve Bennett and County Judge Al Peterson went to lunch at the Italian restaurant just south of downtown. Arriving at the courthouse, James noticed Milton Bastine huffing and puffing up the steps to the second floor, where most of the offices were located. As the county judge excused himself and went to his offices on the first floor, the older attorney glared at them from the staircase. At James, mostly.

James nodded, but didn't initiate a conversation as he and the D.A. took the opposite staircase. The last thing he wanted was to be confronted by an angry fellow attorney whom he might face in court, or need to collaborate with on a future case.

The D.A. went into his offices. In the echoing hallways of the old stone courthouse, James heard Bastine's heavy breathing. The guy should really take the elevator around back.

"How's your girlfriend?" Bastine said in his raspy voice, which sounded oddly threatening in the quiet courthouse.

"What's that supposed to mean?" James said, turning around.

Bastine stood maybe fifteen feet away and sneered. "Nothing." He turned and went into the probation offices.

James didn't like the tone of that comment. He didn't know how the lawyer knew about Scarlett, or even if he did, but he obviously knew that James had a relationship with someone. How jealous was he? James decided to ask the D.A., who probably knew the guy. He changed direction and walked around the corner to Harve's offices.

"Bastine seems to have it in for me," he told him a few minutes later. "He confronted me last week, as you know, but this time, he asked about my girlfriend, as if he knew something."

Harve raised his eyebrow. "What could he know?"

"I'm not keeping any secrets. I've been dating a hairstylist from Atlanta who's on her way to L.A. She had car trouble and got stuck here for a couple of weeks. Her vehicle will probably be ready this week, and she'll be leaving."

Saying the words out loud made her imminent departure seem all too real. "As I said, it's no secret. She's met just about everyone in Brody's Crossing. She even knows my mother!"

"I know he's thinking about running for the county criminal court when Arnold retires. He probably resents you, sees you as a threat. Whatever the reason, we can't have people issuing threats, even veiled, nonspecific ones."

"He's not…unstable, is he?"

"As in, would he hurt you or your girlfriend?"

"Something like that, yeah."

"I don't think so. I'll make sure, though."

"Thanks." James shook the man's hand. "I'll see you tomorrow if not before."

"Right."

He pushed Milton Bastine out of his mind and focused on his judicial responsibilities. As for Scarlett… She would be in Brody's Crossing, safe and sound, when he returned home.

If he didn't believe that, he was going to have to chain her to the heavy wood table in the courtroom so she didn't run away while he was otherwise occupied. Of course, that image led to more sensual thoughts of what he'd do to Scarlett if they had the courtroom to themselves, which shot his concentration all to hell for the rest of the day.

Chapter Thirteen

"Honey, I'm home," James said as he opened the back door of the salon, just after six o'clock. Scarlett looked up from a recent celebrity style magazine that Clarissa subscribed to and smiled at him. "Look. Diego's salon is mentioned in this article on a charity hairstyle event." She turned the publication so he could see the photo of the elegant glass-and-malachite interior. "Isn't it beautiful?"

He didn't look very impressed, but then, he wasn't a stylist, and probably didn't care about how the salon would be viewed by the important clients who entered those doors. "I suppose."

"I can't wait to see it in person."

He didn't say anything, just passed the magazine back to her. Only then did he smile. "Are you ready for dinner? I'm starving."

"Sure. Let me get my shoes on." She felt a little deflated that he couldn't share her enthusiasm, but then she remembered that this was his first day as a judge. "How was Graham? Did anything exciting happen in the courthouse?"

He was silent for a moment, as if he had to think about his answer. "Not really." He walked over and picked up her hoodie from the back of a chair. "Anything exciting happen here?"

"No, just a normal Monday."

He smiled. "Good. That's good."

"Were you expecting something to happen?"

"No! Not at all. Just making conversation."

"Geesh, next we can talk about the weather."

He looked contrite. "Sorry. It's been a long day."

They went to dinner, where conversation seemed to be more normal as James drank a beer and Scarlett had her usual diet soft drink. By the end of the meal, they were holding hands beneath the table, because Scarlett didn't want people to talk about them. James spoiled all her plans by kissing her as he helped her on with the hoodie.

"People will talk," she said, thinking there must be more "Demanding Desmonds" out there in the world.

"I told you I don't care."

But *she* cared, and she hurried out to his SUV. Within minutes they were behind his apartment. He put the vehicle in Park but didn't turn off the engine.

"Stay with me tonight," he said.

She nodded. "You do have a comfortable bed."

He turned the key and smiled. "I knew there was a good reason." He pulled her close and kissed her, and suddenly everything seemed just fine.

ON TUESDAY, James addressed a women's social group in a private area of the Graham tearoom. The decor was frilly, with chintz curtains and tablecloths, flowered china cups and covered cake plates. But his audience was attentive.

James focused his talk on changes to the juvenile codes. His remarks seemed well received by the mostly older ladies, and he was just finishing up when Milton Bastine walked in and took a seat. Even from across the room, the older man radiated hatred.

James fell silent, shocked, as always, by Bastine's strong emotions. James could understand a feeling of entitlement because of his age, but to an elected position? That made no sense. Besides, James hadn't decided to run for office, even though his friend and mentor had encouraged him.

"What, you feeling guilty, Brody?" Bastine called out.

"Mr. Bastine, I have no idea what you're talking about, and besides, I've done nothing to feel guilty about."

"Oh, I doubt that. Just ask that redheaded floozy you're running around naked with."

James heard the gasps from the room at the same time he felt his blood heat and his hands clench.

"That's enough."

"No, it's not! You're just a young pup. You can't come into our courthouse and take over."

"I'm not going to have this conversation with you in this setting, Mr. Bastine. You're upsetting the ladies and you're ruining their lunch."

"Some things are more important than sipping tea and nibbling on little sandwiches. Wise up, ladies, before you invite an immoral womanizer into your midst!"

More gasps followed those idiotic remarks. James opened his phone and dialed 9-1-1. "This is James Brody. There's a disturbed man at the tearoom," he told the operator. "I believe an officer should be dispatched."

"Don't you threaten me, you...you interloper."

"Calm down, Mr. Bastine," James said, walking toward him, hoping he wasn't carrying a weapon. In Texas, that was always a possibility. He hadn't thought to ask Harve to check if Bastine had a concealed-carry permit.

"I'm not waiting around for the police to come. They're

probably on your side, anyway." He leaped from the wooden chair, toppling it. "You think you'll be elected when your old friend retires, but if I can't have that position, I'll make sure you can't, either!" With that, Bastine pushed past the startled manager and several patrons, who'd stopped to listen.

The front door slammed and silence descended over the group.

"Ladies, I am so sorry," James began. "He is obviously angry. Unjustifiably, I might add. As you probably know, no one is appointed to succeed anyone else in the judicial system. This remains a democracy."

He paused and looked at their startled faces. "As for the other accusations…all I can say is that my personal life is just that—personal. I'm dating someone whom I care for a great deal. We are both single people and what we do in the privacy of our homes is our business." Even if they'd been interrupted by people who ran right to Milton Bastine with a "scandal" that fueled his obsession.

The police came, and James excused himself to answer questions for their report. When he'd finished, many of the ladies had left, but some remained.

"We're so sorry for you," one of them said.

"That man has always been an ass," another stated.

"Who would ever vote for him for anything? I doubt his relatives would even support him! Everyone knows he is crazy."

"I'm not sure if he's crazy, but he's angry," James said, "and I'm sorry his feud with me ruined your lunch."

"Why, this is the most exciting luncheon ever!" one of the ladies exclaimed.

I could do without quite as much excitement in my life, James thought as he smiled and prepared to leave.

As he walked toward the front, a very sweet looking elderly lady stopped him with a hand on his arm. "So, you're not going to tell us anything about running around naked?"

"No, ma'am, I'm not."

She sighed and patted his sleeve. "Well, an old lady can hope, if you know what I mean."

After such an adrenaline filled confrontation with Bastine, this lady's remarks lifted James's spirits, but only temporarily. His smile faded as he walked back to the courthouse. He had a lot to take care of this afternoon, including one angry, jealous attorney.

"THE CAR WILL BE READY on Thursday," Claude said, "if the new hoses and belts come in by Wednesday. That's tomorrow. I can't rush them no more than I already am."

"I need to leave, Claude."

"These things take time. I'm hurrying as much as I can."

"Christmas is a week from today! The people who rent apartments might go on vacation, and then I won't have a place to live in L.A." She might end up in a real dump, or something overpriced, because it was all she could find. Or even a hotel, which would waste more of her money.

"I'm sorry. Maybe you need to spend Christmas right here."

Scarlett felt like pounding her forehead on Claude's grimy counter. "I'm starting my new job on January 2. I'm running out of time."

"Christmas in Brody's Crossing is mighty fine."

She shook her head. Why couldn't she make Claude— or anyone, for that matter— understand? Her new life was in California. Life here in Brody's Crossing wasn't real, even if it did feel that way so often lately. Even if it did seem more and more as if she belonged.

Especially when she woke up in James's arms, in his bed. When they laughed together. When he kissed her...

She sighed. "Just do your best, please."

"Yes, ma'am, I surely will."

Scarlett walked back to the salon, hugging her arms around her. She had to leave. She wanted to stay. How had she let herself get into such a quandary? As much as some people wanted to think she was wild and unfocused, she'd always had goals. James knew that about her. He admired her.

And she was going to leave him.

How could she achieve her dream and have James, too? She couldn't. He'd made it clear that he would never leave Brody's Crossing. Not even if he loved her.

"Scarlett, are you okay?" Clarissa asked. She stood at the back room counter, pouring a cup of coffee.

"No, not really," Scarlett said, plopping down on the couch. "I just checked on my car. It should be ready on Thursday. That's good, I suppose, considering the rest of the parts won't be here until tomorrow. And I really need to get to L.A. before everyone leaves for Christmas. It's just that..."

"What, hon?"

"I'm going to be leaving a lot behind." She felt like crying, like giving in to the emotions she normally kept in check. This time, she couldn't make a joke or change the subject. She was too upset.

"It's James, isn't it?"

"Of course. I told myself not to let this happen, yet here I am, caring too much. Letting myself fall for him when there's no future for us."

"I don't know why you thought you could avoid falling for him. Why, he's just perfect for you, and you're perfect for him."

"How can you say that? We're as different as can be."

"Maybe you seem different, but that's what makes things interesting. You're two halves of a whole."

"Clarissa, if I don't go to L.A., I'll be missing what might be the chance of a lifetime."

"To work in a fancy salon out there."

"Well, yes."

"So you can do hair for rich people who are convinced they're more important than the rest of us."

"That's rather cynical, isn't it? I'm sure many of them are very nice."

"Might be, but I doubt it. Scarlett, you're not going to be their friend. You'll be doing a job for them, and they'll pay you and tip you just like everyone else, and when they leave, or when you go and do their hair and *you* leave, they'll forget about you." Clarissa came over and took her hands. "What I'm saying is that those people aren't your friends. They're not your family. They'll never be close to you. That's a fact of life."

Scarlett felt tears and drew in a deep breath. "I'm not expecting them to be my friends. I just want to be recognized. I want to create. I want to be a part of that whole industry. It's so exciting, Clarissa. Can't you see that?"

"Yes, I can see that, but is being in an exciting place the most important thing in life? Does fame and fortune trump friends and family? I don't think so, sweetie."

Scarlett dropped her head between her hands and closed her eyes. "I'm so confused."

"Do you love him that much?"

"I don't know! I like him an awful lot. But I've never been in love before. How do I tell for certain?"

"Sweetie, I think you know, but you're sure fighting hard not to." Clarissa rubbed Scarlett's back, then said, "I hate to heap more on you when you've got so much on your mind, but something happened today in Graham that I think you should know about."

Scarlett's head popped up. "What? Is it James? Is he okay?"

Clarissa smiled. "That's how you know you're in love." She waved her hand. "But he's fine. It's about him, though. Some crazy old attorney from Graham, Milton Bastine, confronted James at a lunchtime speaking engagement."

"What do you mean, confronted? As in assaulted?"

"No, just verbal stuff. The silly old geiser is jealous of James. He wants to run for the judgeship—the criminal court where James is serving. Apparently the fact that James was asked to sit in during the judge's absence pushed him over the edge. He's convinced that James is taking something away from him."

"That's irrational, unless he was promised something."

"That old coot wasn't promised a thing. You can't 'promise' something like that, since to get the job, he'd have to run for office. Now, way back when, lots of under the table deals were made. But that was a long time ago. Even in small towns, those kinds of things get brought to light."

"I can't understand why he would blame James!"

Clarissa shrugged. "Apparently he thinks James is just as devious and underhanded as he is. He must believe James got the judge to ask him to sit in, in some scheme to take over."

"Where did you hear this?"

"From a client friend of mine who was there. She told me it was quite heated. That Bastine even accused James of running around naked! And Scarlett, I know this is going to bother you, but you're going to find out one way or another. The old coot specifically said he was running around with a redheaded floozy."

"What! How would he know… Why would he say that?"

"I'm not sure. He must know that you and James are dating, but I don't know how, since Bastine doesn't live in Brody's Crossing."

"That's creepy!"

"James called the police."

"The police!" When Scarlett thought about what the man had said… Could he know something about Sunday morning at the ranch? Why else would he say *that*?

If she'd caused James any problems, she would feel so bad. James knew she was worried about their relationship affecting his status in the community, but he'd told her not to worry. He'd told her that they weren't doing anything wrong.

She shouldn't have taken off her clothes in the barn. Where was her sense?

"Don't worry, hon. James will take care of it."

How could he take care of rumors that were true?

SCARLETT TALKED TO JAMES by phone later in the afternoon, letting him know that the news was out about the lunchtime altercation. He was concerned, but not too much. Or so it seemed. Maybe he was being brave for her. Maybe the accusations really bothered him. She wanted to see him, to watch his face as he explained what had happened. Only then would she truly know how he was feeling.

She finished up her last appointment, a cut and style of Bobbie Jean Maxwell's highlighted classic bob. She was a nice lady who advised Scarlett to give this little scandal time to blow over. She also said to let James handle everything. After all, it was his reputation being besmirched. But that was hard advice for Scarlett to follow. *She* wanted to do something to help, directly and dramatically.

Like punch Milton Bastine in the nose. Probably not a good idea.

Venetia returned from the bank, red-faced and stomping. "Is the weather getting worse?" Scarlett asked.

"No! It's this damn storm of gossip about what happened in Graham. People who don't even know you and James want to put their spin on the tale. Just now, someone asked me if you were a floozy! They wanted to know if you ran around naked! Can you imagine such nonsense?"

"No, I can honestly say I never thought I'd be called a nudist floozy." Besides sounding horribly old-fashioned, "floozy" meant she used men to get what she wanted. Nothing could be further from the truth.

"I've been advised to do everything from turn the other cheek to march to Milton Bastine's law office and demand an apology," Scarlett said. "I have no idea what to do to help James. I'm not concerned about me."

"We're concerned about both of you," Clarissa said, walking out of the back room, where she'd been washing a load of towels. "Personally, I like the idea of marching on the old coot's office."

"Yeah," Venetia said, "too bad we don't have a floozy union, or we could organize and strike."

Clarissa stopped and rubbed her chin. "A floozy union. I like that." She ran to the back and started opening cabinets. Venetia and Scarlett both followed her to see what she was up to.

She stood in front of the supplies for coloring hair. "Girls, I have an idea," she said with an evil twinkle in her blue eyes.

JAMES WENT BY THE SALON. To his surprise, the lights were all on and Clarissa's and Venetia's cars were still there. "What's up, ladies?" he asked as he let himself in the back door.

All three of the women looked guilty, even though they

weren't doing anything unusual. His brain was too tired at the moment to dissect their actions. All he wanted was a good meal, a quiet evening and a good night's sleep with Scarlett by his side.

"Nothing! We're just…taking inventory," Clarissa announced. "Venetia and I were almost finished here, weren't we, Scarlett."

"I believe so."

"Scarlett, would you like to come to my place for dinner?" James asked. "I really don't feel like going out and answering any more questions."

"Of course, but—"

"Don't worry. We'll finish up here," Clarissa said.

"If you're sure …"

"We're sure. We have everything we need, right?"

"Yes, we do," Venetia replied.

"We'll see you in the morning," Clarissa told Scarlett. "And don't forget our Christmas lunch and our little after-lunch excursion."

"Of course. I'm ready."

"We'll be ready, too," Clarissa said. "Now, you and James run along. I'll lock up."

Scarlett snagged her hoodie and followed him to the back door. "You're sure?" she asked before they went outside.

"Yes!" Clarissa answered. "Now, have a good time."

James opened the door for Scarlett, then drove the block and a half to his building. He parked in his usual spot out back and climbed the outside stairs, all the while thinking that the colorful pixie in front of him didn't deserve such disrespect. People took one look at her bright red hair, colorful clothes and twinkling belly button ring, and assumed she was a little wild.

When they'd first met, he himself had made some assumptions about her. That she didn't care what others thought. That she would give everyone a lot of attitude, no matter what the situation.

She wasn't any of those things. Scarlett was sweet and vulnerable, funny and smart. He could spend a lot of years discovering all her nuances.

He placed his briefcase on the kitchen table, loosened his tie and sighed. "Would you like a drink?"

"Maybe a glass of wine, if you have some."

"Sure. Take a look at what I have," he said, motioning toward the wine rack. "I'm going to change clothes and then I'll start dinner." He walked over, hugged her and whispered, "I missed you today."

"I...I thought about you, too," she admitted.

He changed into jeans and his UT sweatshirt, then walked back into the kitchen. Scarlett had found a CD she liked, and was struggling to open a bottle of pinot grigio.

"Would you like some help?"

"Sure. I don't do this often."

He took the bottle from her. "You're not a big drinker."

"No, not really. I've never liked the taste of liquor."

"You don't sleep around, either." He inserted the corkscrew, pushed the arms down to raise the cork.

"No, I don't." She held out a glass.

"And you're really sweet." He poured her wine.

"What are you trying to say?"

James set the bottle on the counter and hugged Scarlett, kissing her temple. "Just making the point that no matter what anyone says about you, you're a fine person. I think maybe you had a little problem with assigning blame. It's not your fault. None of this is your fault. We're going to place the blame where it should be—on Milton Bastine. I'm not sure what exactly pushed him over the edge, and maybe it's not really important, but I intend to stop him from harassing either of us."

"No one should mess with your career like this, as if they had the right to talk about you."

"How about you? I don't want you to feel the least little amount of guilt over what happened in my parent's barn."

"I can't help but feel a little sorry that I…well, I took my clothes off. I'm the reason that woman was able to talk about us that way. But I'm working on it. I have a plan."

"A plan. Yes…to make me feel better." He hugged her again. "I'm all for goals and plans, except when they take you away from me."

"I know." She turned in his arms. "But we all must follow our destiny, right? You knew it was right to come back to Brody's Crossing. If you hadn't followed your dream to be an attorney in your hometown, I'm sure you would have felt disappointed."

"Yes, you're right. But I'm asking you now, in light of what has happened between us, if you'll reconsider your goal of moving to California. Is there anyway you could see yourself here, in Brody's Crossing?"

She pulled away, turned and paced to the window. "Working in a small-town salon isn't my dream. That's something that hasn't changed from the day I rode into town on that Christmas tree truck."

He paused as he felt his heart rip. "Okay, then." He poured himself a glass of wine, then walked to where Scarlett stood by the window. "I'll fix dinner now.".

"I can help."

"Okay. That would be great." He started to turn away, but she caught his sleeve.

"Even if I can accept the idea that Bastine is to blame, I'm still sorry all this happened."

"I know. I'm sorry, too."

He fixed frozen chicken pot pies—one of his favorite comfort foods—and Scarlett mixed a pan of brownies for dessert. As the food baked, they drank another glass of wine and he told her about his meeting with the D.A. after lunch. They'd discovered the connection between Joan Lindell and Milton Bastine. Joan was his former step-daughter. Apparently Bastine was divorced, but Joan didn't get along with her mother. She sided with her former step-father, whom she saw as a tragic character.

That, combined with many people's opinion that Joan was just as nutty as Milton, made a very bad situation worse.

James hadn't told anyone that the whole "naked" part of the accusation was true. That was no one's business. The only thing he regretted was that they'd been interrupted. He'd never regret making love to Scarlett in the fragrant hay, in the crisp winter air.

If he had the opportunity again, he'd do the same thing. Only this time, if he was interrupted, he'd tell those old biddies to get their trespassing selves off the property, red velvet cake and all.

Chapter Fourteen

They went to bed early and made sweet love, but when he awoke, Scarlett was once again gone. Today, however, he was fairly certain she would be here when he got back home. Tomorrow, he wasn't so sure… After all, Claude said her car would be ready Thursday, and she'd made it clear that she was leaving as soon as the Benz could make the trip to California.

James had asked her twice to stay. Once, just through the holiday. Last night, he'd asked her to stay in Brody's Crossing. He would try one more time tonight.

Maybe he hadn't said the right words. In all the chaos that was his professional and personal life, perhaps he could figure this out while he was away from Scarlett today, because time was running out.

CLARISSA INSISTED that she could take care of most of the planning for their day. Scarlett concentrated on calming herself, putting together the little gifts she'd purchased for the "girls" for their Christmas lunch, and doing the hair of several people.

If she never saw red hair coloring again, it would be too

soon. She was going to be a blonde or a brunette as soon as possible. Maybe she'd even change her name.

The weather was mild and breezy. They put the Closed sign in the window of the salon and walked around the corner to the café. Bobbi Jean Maxwell, Ida Bell and even Carolyn Brody were already there, grinning and causing quite a commotion in the restaurant.

As Scarlett looked around, she saw clients and other people she'd met in the past two weeks. They had apparently decided to join the party, wearing hats of all types. Sisters, mothers and daughters, they all looked at her expectantly. Suddenly, she felt tears well in her eyes. And the five little gifts she'd purchased for the immediate lunch group didn't seem at all adequate to express her feelings for everyone who'd shown up.

BY THE TIME Scarlett and the group left the café, everyone was revved up. They piled into Ida's van and Clarissa's sedan and a half-dozen other cars, then made phone calls to some more people who were meeting them in Graham.

Scarlett was on a mission to save the man she loved. It was the least she could do before she left town tomorrow. She would at least know that he'd been shown how much his friends and neighbors cared for him. Once she was gone, he'd have the support and love of all these women and their families. If any small-minded people believed a jealous lawyer—well, they didn't matter at all.

"EXCUSE ME, MR. BRODY, but did you know that Milton Bastine was holding a press conference at the Confederate memorial at two o'clock this afternoon?"

James looked up at the court secretary. "Press conference? For one thing, what the heck does he need to say?

And who gave him the right to use public property for his press conference?"

"I'm not sure if he has a permit. Would you like for me to check?"

"Yes, and tell the police chief that I'd like to speak to him, also, before he does anything." James had a feeling that Bastine would like nothing more than to have his little press party interrupted by the police, called by James, so he could complain that his freedom of speech was being thwarted.

After a short while, James spoke to the police, who promised to have a few officers on hand. But they wouldn't stop the press conference unless it went on too long or caused a public nuisance. James sat at his desk, looked out the window at the south end of the courthouse, and wondered what Scarlett was doing.

The vision of her packing invaded his thoughts, and he went back to reading a recent appeals court decision.

At a few minutes before two o'clock, he shrugged into his suit coat, adjusted his tie and checked his cuffs. He used the mirror in the hallway to smooth his hair, which was now tamed and parted as it had been before Scarlett arrived.

He had a strong urge to ruffle it, spike it, do something different. Scarlett's influence, do doubt.

On the way out the door, he stopped at the secretary's desk. "Any calls I need to take care of before I go out?"

"No calls."

"Thanks, Mary." Steeling himself against showing anger toward Bastine, he went down the worn stone stairs and out the front door.

Bastine was pacing in front of the marble obelisk dedicated to the Confederate dead from the county. He had attracted only a small crowd. The *Graham Leader*, probably in response to the lunchtime incident yesterday, had a reporter and photographer in attendance. James sincerely hoped this wasn't going to turn into a circus. The two officers standing off to the side by the parking lot would hopefully see to that.

Bastine started to speak—not very eloquently or professionally, in James's opinion. The outrageous anger of yesterday was gone. Maybe Milton had taken some medication. In any case, he didn't seem so crazy today. He said he was an upstanding, long-time member of the community. He was going to run in opposition to the current district judge in the next primary. He had right on his side. Yada, yada, yada. James suppressed a yawn.

Then Bastine claimed he would fight the forces of corruption, in the form of political favors, or even if they entered the county in the form of redheaded Jezebels.

Okay, now he was getting personal.

The reporter from the *Leader* asked him what he meant by that remark, and Milton began to describe women who tempted even the most respectable men. James clenched his fists and took a step forward.

If that blowhard said one word about Scarlett, he would take him out—cameras, police, reporters or no.

Before Bastine could continue to pontificate, or the reporter could ask more questions, James heard numerous car doors slam from the east side of the square. He looked to his right and blinked.

A group of women, all of them with bright red hair and even brighter clothes, assembled on the sidewalk. As they marched toward him, they raised signs and began to chant, "We love James."

The reporter turned and watched, and the photographer focused his digital camera, while the police came to attention with their hands on their nightsticks. The women attracted a crowd, who walked behind them as they approached Bastine's press conference.

One of the redheads, whom James knew was Clarissa, flipped her bright pink feather boa around her neck and spoke directly to Bastine. "We're all redheaded floozys who love James Brody."

"Yes, we do!" several more women chorused.

"And we don't want to hear one more bad word about him cross your lips," she said, pointing her finger at the shocked, flushed older lawyer. "If we do, we'll all come over to your place and give you a good spanking." She turned to the other ladies. "Isn't that right, girls?"

They all sang out, "Spank, spank, spank."

Bastine's face turned even more red. The reporter from the *Leader* cracked a smile, and even the police officers looked as if they wanted to laugh.

"James is the best man we know," Myra Hammer said, "even if he won't sue whoever we want him to sue. If he did, he'd be rich!"

"That's right! He cares about our town and this county," Ida Bell added.

"He's the best!" James's mother exclaimed. His mother? James looked closer and saw she wore a tight purple sweater and a bright yellow skirt. Had he seen that on a cheerleader once? She'd accessorized with a purple boa and lots of long beads.

"We don't want to hear one more lie or innuendo about James Brody," Scarlett—the real Scarlett—said. "If we do, you'll be subject to another attack of the redheaded floozys."

The crowd began to laugh, surrounding the women so they could get a better look. Some people took photos of the "floozys" with their cell phone cameras. Bastine tried to speak, tried to get their attention, but no one wanted to hear any more of his nonsense.

In the middle of the group, Scarlett stood as tall as her petite frame would allow. She got lots of hugs and seemed to relish the attention, unlike the time she'd styled Hailey's hair. Then, she'd run from praise. Now, she accepted it gracefully.

If only she'd be here forever to protect his backside. Was that what she was trying to tell him? Suddenly, he wanted to get her alone, to ask her if she'd changed her mind. But the redheads advanced and enveloped him in hugs until he began to laugh.

The last thing he saw was Milton Bastine slinking off to his car without another comment.

When James looked around for Scarlett, she was gone. He wanted to run find her. What if she'd left for good? He grabbed Clarissa and asked, "Where is she?"

"Hon, she's fine. She'll be waiting for you."

"How do you know for sure? She could be heading for Weatherford to catch a bus right now. Or maybe Claude got her car done and she's on the road to California."

"She's not headed anywhere. For one thing, she knows that car will be ready tomorrow. And just to make sure, I bribed Claude with six months' worth of haircuts and manicures—and believe me, that was a real sacrifice on my part, if you've ever seen his hands—to keep those keys away from Scarlett."

"Oh. Good thinking." James wished he'd been that manipulative.

"The thing is, Scarlett needs a real good reason to stay in our little town, now that she feels she's done everything she had to before she says goodbye."

Hadn't he given her a good reason to stay? No, he hadn't.

That was on his to-do list for today: find out where he went wrong when he'd asked her to stay before. And suddenly, James knew what he had to do so she'd *never* say goodbye.

SCARLETT BUMMED A RIDE back to Brody's Crossing with Myra Hammer, who declared the post-demonstration too sappy for her. She'd said what she wanted to say, and now she was ready to go home, even though it was only mid-afternoon.

Scarlett hadn't wanted to stay around to answer questions. Once she knew that James was okay, she felt free to leave. With Myra, of all people!

Myra was one strange woman, but Scarlett was glad that, for all her complaining about James not suing on demand, Myra had stood up for him.

Just like so many other women. And they'd all dyed their hair! Granted, the rinses were temporary, and the color would fade after about four washes, but it was still a huge gesture.

She smiled as she recalled the wild clothes. They'd raided the thrift stores, their daughters' closets and even the church charity clothing stash. They'd certainly done their best to look like floozys.

"You're awful cheerful for someone who's leaving here tomorrow."

"How do you know that?"

"Claude told my husband Bud at the Burger Barn yesterday. He said your car parts came in. I guess you'll be on the road, driving away from all of us as fast as you can."

"It's not like that, Myra. I have a job to go to."

"You've got a job here!"

"Clarissa gave me a job, and I know she was short one stylist, but that doesn't mean she wants *me* permanently."

"Oh, don't be silly. Of course she does."

"This job in L.A. is a dream opportunity. I might never get a chance like this again."

"Oh, pshaw. A job's a job. When are you gonna find another man like James Brody?"

Scarlett didn't have an answer for that, at least one that she cared to share. So she gazed out the windshield at the winter-brown landscape, the hills and occasional mesas, with their flat tops and steep sides. They were fascinating and so different from the rocky formations in Georgia. If she thought of them enough, she wouldn't remember that James would be back in town late this afternoon, expecting an explanation.

"I think you should stay and have James sue that Bastine character. He said all kinds of negative things about you."

"I'm not sure I can sue someone for expressing an opinion about me."

"Oh, you sound just like James!"

Scarlett didn't have anything to say to that comment, so she turned her head as they drove by the retro-style, boarded-up Sweet Dreams Motel and several newer businesses. Then they drove past McCaskie's, where her Benz was inside the bay, getting repaired.

Myra stopped across from the salon. "If you make the mistake of leaving tomorrow, you have a good trip, and be careful. When that car breaks down, you might not find such nice people again to help you out."

"Thanks, Myra. I'll remember that."

Scarlett trudged across the street. Darn the gloomy old biddy, but she was right. If the Benz had broken down in some other place, Scarlett might have been stranded without friends or a roof over her head.

She let herself into the salon with the key Clarissa had given her. Trusted her with. Without turning on the lights,

Scarlett walked to the room she'd used for the past two and a half weeks.

Under different circumstances, she might have been forced to abandon her car, fly to L.A. or, heaven forbid, back to Atlanta. She might have been taken advantage of, attacked or worse. She might have been forced to call her parents, her brother or sister for help.

Instead, she'd been welcomed, given a place to stay, wined and dined by the town's most eligible bachelor, invited to participate in community activities, and offered friendship by people from all ages and backgrounds.

And she was going to give all that up to move to California to work in Diego's trendy salon. For the opportunity to *perhaps* become a popular stylist. For the chance she *might* work on celebrity clients.

The move was a huge gamble. How many others tried and failed?

But if she didn't try, wouldn't she always regret her decision? That's what career counselors, other stylists and her friends in general told her. "Go for it!" had been the prevailing cheer when she told people about Diego's job offer.

Besides, James had never said exactly how he felt about her. He'd never told her, for example, that he was madly and passionately in love with her. That he couldn't live without her. No, he'd just asked her to stay and work here. As if that was enough!

Well, it wasn't. Life was more than work. Life was… Oh, my God. Life was more than work! She was only moving to California because of work.

But she would only stay for love.

JAMES DROVE BY THE SALON, which was dark inside except for a light in the back room. A sign said they were closed for the afternoon. Since he'd seen Scarlett's car at the garage earlier, he knew she hadn't left town. Reassured that she hadn't fled, he went to his apartment.

Within a few minutes he'd changed into jeans, a long-sleeved polo and athletic shoes. He hit the stairs at a jog and arrived at the back door of the salon just slightly out of breath, the Christmas gift bag from the store in Graham, plus another one he'd bought at the convenience store, clutched in his hand.

The door was locked, so he knocked, but he didn't have to wait long for her to open it. She had apparently been in the shower, because she was wrapped in a fluffy spa-type robe with a white towel turban-style around her head.

"Hi," she said, looking rather shy. Without the wild spikes of red hair and her normal eye makeup, her face appeared so different. Softer, younger, more vulnerable.

"Hi to you," he replied. "May I come in?"

"Oh, of course." She moved back and he stepped inside, close enough to smell the soap and shampoo and whatever else she used to soften that beautiful skin.

"I bought you something last week. I knew it would be either a Christmas present or a going away gift. I wasn't sure which."

She looked at the bag and nodded. "Would you like to sit down?"

"That might be a good idea."

They walked to the sofa. She sat on one end and clutched a pillow to her chest, as though she needed to protect her heart. Perhaps she felt as if she did. He hoped the feeling was fleeting.

"The thing is, I decided it wasn't quite right for you. Especially not after today."

She bit her bottom lip. "Did it… What happened after I left?"

James smiled. "I suppose you saw Milton Bastine run for his car. After that, Clarissa became the star, giving interviews to the newspaper and telling people a wonderfully romantic story about a stranded young woman who found a place to stay during Christmastime."

"Clarissa can spin a good tale."

James nodded. "I think with your dramatic demonstration, the point was made. I doubt we'll hear any more from disgruntled lawyers or nosy old biddies. I'm sure the article in the *Leader* will be fact-based. Plus, they'll have those photos."

"Ah, yes. I'd like to see those."

James moved closer, gently removed the pillow from Scarlett's arms and framed her face with his hands. "You'll have to stay in order to see those photos."

"I know." She paused and pulled his hands down to hold hers. Her fingers were cold as he wrapped her in his heat. "I'd planned to leave tomorrow," she finally said, "but my plans aren't firm."

James smiled again. "That's good, because I think I finally figured this out."

She tilted her head. The towel turban threatened to slip off, and she adjusted it while he retrieved the two bags.

"This first very tasteful bag is what I bought for you either for Christmas, if I could talk you into staying, or as a going away gift, in case you decided to leave for California before the twenty-fifth." He held up a dark green bag with a dangling pinecone and plaid ribbons. "Very nice package."

"Yes, very tasteful."

He held up the other bag, one with a jovial Frosty the Snowman, chirping cardinals and scampering bunnies, with cartoonish evergreens in the background. He'd paid all of a dollar for the bag, and it showed. "Not as tasteful," he admitted.

"I suppose not."

"I bought it today. There's another gift inside. The thing is, you have to choose."

"Just based on the gift bag?"

"No, I don't suppose that would be fair, would it?" He sat the bags on the couch and took her hands again. "Today, when you and the other 'floozys' marched on the court-house, I wasn't sure what was up. As usual, you had me guessing. I've never really known anyone like you. I never thought I could have a relationship with a woman when I didn't even know her name."

He paused, then resisted the urge to pull her close and stop talking, because he wasn't sure if his words would be right. If they would be enough.

"I didn't realize until after the event was finished that I'd never really asked you the right question. All of a sudden, I saw the situation from your perspective. I knew that I was asking you to make a life-altering decision without all the information."

"What information?" she whispered.

He looked at their joined hands, then back into her cautious, hopeful green eyes. "I love you. I love you with-out knowing your real name, without any assurances that you'll be here tomorrow, without any promises or expec-tations. I love you because I do, and there's not a thing you could do to change how I feel."

"Oh, James," she started to say, but then her eyes filled with tears. James felt himself blinking, too. He looked down at the bags, then let go of her hands to hold them up.

"The thing is, you can have this tasteful gift, or you can

take a chance on what's in this silly bag. It will be a surprise, but it comes with my heart."

"If it comes with your heart, that's the one I want." She reached for the second bag, but he held on.

"This is the gift I should have given you, regardless of Christmas or your leaving or anything, because it comes with my love."

She reached into the bag and pulled out a box, then opened it. Inside was a jewelers box. Scarlett gasped a little as she opened the hinged lid.

A delicate engagement ring and wedding band nestled together on white velvet. The ring reminded him of Scarlett because of the star-shaped setting, the combination of round and marquis diamonds and the small rubies nestled between. The band alternated diamonds and rubies.

"It's a set. I'm willing to give you time, but this is for a wedding, not just an engagement. I wanted you to know that. I'm looking for forever. With you."

"Oh, James," she sighed again.

He took the engagement ring out of the box. "Will you accept this, knowing that it means you'll be stuck here in Brody's Crossing forever, even after you get your car repaired? Even if you have a great job waiting for you in California?"

"I thought a lot about us. About what I wanted. I realized that the dream job in L.A. was just that—a dream. I never dealt with the reality of the situation. I wanted to move out there, get celebrity clients, and be able to tell my family how successful I was."

Scarlett shook her head and the turban slipped again. "That wasn't a very mature attitude, I know, but I think I was reacting as a child. Not as an adult. Once I got here, people treated me as an individual. It was amazing. It was…liberating. For the first time in my life, I truly feel like a grown-up."

"Sometimes it takes a while," he murmured. "When I married before, it was because I thought the time was right, the bride was right. We had the right kinds of jobs and life was supposed to be great. Then I discovered what was really important to me, and climbing the ladder of success wasn't it."

"The same thing happened to me in Brody's Crossing. Here, I became an adult. Here, I learned to love."

"The town?"

Scarlett laughed. "No, you! I love you."

He wrapped her in his arms, holding her tight. "Did you just figure that out?"

"No, I knew days ago." She pulled back a little and wiped another tear from her eye. "I knew right away that I was falling in love with you, but I tried really hard not to. I knew I was leaving. I told myself you'd break my heart."

"I would never break your heart."

"When you asked me twice to stay, you never said you loved me. You only said you wanted me around."

He held her close again. "I'm sorry, Scarlett. I wasn't expecting to fall in love. I didn't recognize our love until I was forced to focus on what was truly important to me. And trust me, it wasn't my career, or sitting on the bench this week, or anything that Milton Bastine could threaten. It was you, and this community, and my family. You're a part of us, Scarlett. You belong here forever."

"Then I'll stay right here, with you."

He slipped the engagement ring on her finger. It was too large, and they'd have to take it back to get it sized, but for now, they sat and admired the sparkle. Scarlett wrapped a rubber band around the shank so the ring wouldn't fall off her hand, then twined her arms around his neck.

"I love you, James Brody. Let's get married."

"Anytime you say." He kissed her, giving her all the love he had inside, holding her tight and touching her everywhere he could reach. The robe parted and the towel fell to the floor as their kisses became hotter, as a sense of urgency overtook them.

"Should we pull out the sofa bed?" she asked between kisses.

"No. Too lumpy." And he went on kissing her.

His clothes were peeled away and her robe parted. At the last minute, he remembered protection, and held up the packet. "Do we need this?"

She drew in a deep breath. "For now, I think. Maybe not too much longer."

"Whatever you think, but you need to know I want a family. Children, when you're ready."

"You'll be a wonderful father," she said, stroking his jaw. "I just don't want to give my family any reason to count the months from our wedding to the birth of our first child."

James smiled. "Fair enough."

Their kisses turned tender, the urgency tempered as they made love on Clarissa's back room sofa. The position was awkward, but he silently promised that next time, they'd be in his comfortable bed once again. And then he thought no more of the awkward position or less-than-private setting as they soared together, sharing their love.

Much later, he lifted his head and shifted on the couch so Scarlett wasn't bearing all of his weight. The sun was setting, but he could still see her in the waning light. He smiled as he ran his fingers over her delicate features, then through her…brown hair?

He lifted a little more, looked again. Yes, her hair was brown. A lovely, warm shade of brown, with red and gold strands.

She opened her eyes. "I took the color out."

"I see that. You're a brunette."

She rolled her eyes. "Like that should have been a surprise to you."

It took him a moment to realize what she was implying, and then he couldn't stop his blush. "Honestly, I never thought about…it. I mean, I didn't really think about the color of—"

She laughed and pulled him down. "You're so cute when you're embarrassed."

"Yeah, but don't mention that to anyone else, okay? I'm supposed to be one tough attorney. My legal opponents should tremble in their wingtips."

Scarlett giggled. "You're a pussycat and everyone in town knows it."

"I'm a tiger. A shark," he claimed, acting indignant.

"You're my tiger," she said, and kissed him again. They didn't come up for air for a long time.

Later, when the room was dark and the night silent, Scarlett asked, "What's in the other bag?"

"Tonight, you just get me. And the ring."

She seemed to think about it a minute, then nodded. "That's enough for me."

Epilogue

James's parents had been wonderful about welcoming her into the family. Scarlett glanced around the cozy kitchen, where she and James had looked out of the bay window and eaten breakfast, and knew that she'd finally found the place where she belonged. Maybe not in this exact house, maybe not on a ranch right now, but in the greater community filled with family and friends.

And hope for the future. She was working her way into a partnership with Clarissa and would eventually buy out the older lady when she was ready to retire. In the meantime, Scarlett was working on retiring the pink smocks.

Carolyn Brody came back to check the sausage pinwheels she'd made for an appetizer, before they ate a belated Christmas dinner a little later today. Christmas had actually been four days before, but since Scarlett's parents were here now, they were celebrating again.

"My father isn't giving James a hard time, is he?" she asked Carolyn.

"No, not at all. You know James. He can talk to anyone.

I think your parents are quite taken with him, if I do say so myself."

Scarlett smiled. "They're probably glad to have a lawyer in the family, since they already have a doctor and an accountant."

"And a stylist," his mother reminded her.

"Yeah, but there's not much demand for that in my family."

"I don't know. I heard you give your mother some advice on her hair." Carolyn leaned close. "Much needed, I might add. You could do wonders with her style."

Scarlett laughed. James poked his head in the doorway. "Are you about ready? We want to open gifts."

"Sure. Let me put these on a tray and we'll be right in." The pinwheels smelled absolutely delicious as Carolyn removed them from the baking sheets. Maybe James's mother would teach her to bake things that didn't come from a mix.

Scarlett grabbed a tray of carrots, celery and broccoli with ranch dressing—another staple Texas finger food she loved—and carried it into the living room. Carolyn followed with the sausage pinwheels.

They settled next to their men. Scarlett curled up on the floor near the tree so she could pass out gifts, while James sat in a dining chair dragged into the living room. He smiled and plopped her Santa hat on her brown curls. The red had all come out, and she'd added just a tiny touch of strawberry-blond highlights around her face.

The white Christmas lights sparkled on the diamond-and-ruby engagement ring, now sized properly and looking right at home on her finger. She smiled whenever she saw it. She couldn't wait to add the ruby-and-diamond band. They'd set the wedding date in April, when James claimed Texas came alive with wildflowers and green grass and endless blue skies. She didn't care as long as they were together, but she humored him because it was important to him that she love Texas.

She passed out gifts and received some from her parents and siblings. As usual, they tried to be practical, and succeeded marginally. How many gloves, scarves, slippers and wallets did one person need? They might never completely understand her, but she was learning to live with that. Maybe someday she'd let them know more about who she was rather than being so defensive.

Maybe the first step would be to use her real name. She was about to make the big announcement when James handed her a familiar dark green gift bag with a pinecone embellishment.

"I thought I wasn't getting this gift?" she said.

"You couldn't have it *then*. Now you can."

She tore out the tissue and reached inside for a white cardboard box. She removed the lid to see a pretty silver sun smiling at her. The long silver chain would look perfect with her sweaters. It was something she would have chosen for herself, and she was touched that he knew her so well.

James leaned close, whispering so only she could hear. "I bought it when I became obsessed with that belly button ring. You know, the moon and star." She nodded. "At the time, I fantasized about seeing you naked, wearing the sun, moon and stars and nothing else." He kissed her neck, just below her ear. "I still do."

She sure wished he wouldn't say things like that when other people were around. All she wanted to do was jump him now, and she still had to sit through dinner with her parents and his! "Hold that thought," she whispered.

"Hey, you two aren't newlyweds yet," her father joked.

James's father laughed. "They get that way," he said. His

speech was only slightly slurred. She'd really started to like his quiet ways. He'd taken her around the barn one Sunday afternoon and told her the names of all the animals.

Carolyn Brody sprang up from her chair. "Appetizers, anyone?"

"Oh, wait. First, I have something to say." Scarlett stood and gave James's hand a squeeze. This was going to be harder than she'd thought. "When I came here, I was simply Scarlett. No last name. I was never happy with my first or middle name. Sorry, Mom, but being named after an old lady in a black robe was a little much."

"It's a nice name! A meaningful name!" Her mother turned to the Brodys. "We named all our children after people we admired, people who were successful in their professions. Our oldest is Jonas Salk Hancock, and he's a doctor, and our other daughter is Margaret Mead Hancock, but she ended up being an accountant rather than a scientist And then—"

"Yeah, well, it wasn't me," Scarlett said, interrupting before her mother said the dreaded name. "Or at least, it wasn't the me I was trying to be. It took this trip and getting stranded here in Brody's Crossing to figure out who I really am."

She paused and took a deep breath. "The truth is, I'm not Scarlett anymore." She fluffed her brown hair. "The color is gone and so is the persona. I'm not going to California to be a stylist to the stars, because I've found the place where I belong."

This was the hard part. "So, from now on, I want all of you to know that you can call me by my real name..." she swallowed and felt a little nauseous "...Sandra Day Hancock."

The room was silent for a long moment, then James started to laugh. "You were supposed to be an attorney and a Supreme Court judge?"

"Hey, this isn't funny," she said, and swatted his arm. At least she was marrying an attorney who would someday, probably, be a judge.

He pulled her onto his lap and wrapped his arms around her, likely so she wouldn't swat him again. "Darlin'," he said in a heavy Texas drawl, "you might be named after an old lady in a black robe, but to me, you'll always be the red-hot love of my life, Scarlett."

He kissed her in front of her parents and his, until his father chuckled and hers cleared his throat. "And come April, you'll be a Brody. You can be Sandra Day Hancock Brody, or Sandra Brody, or Sandy Brody or Scarlett Brody. Or you can reinvent yourself however you like, just as long as you remember that we belong together."

She fumed for a moment, then put her arms around his neck. "Okay, I'll think about it," she agreed, and kissed him back.

She was beginning to feel more and more like a soft, lovable Sandy and less like a hard-edged Scarlett by the minute, and that was just fine with her.

* * * * *

Turn the page for a sneak preview
of the first book in the new miniseries
DIAMONDS DOWN UNDER
from Silhouette Desire®,
VOWS & A VENGEFUL GROOM
by Bronwyn Jameson

Available January 2008

Silhouette Desire®
Always Powerful, Passionate and Provocative

Kimberley Blackstone didn't notice the waiting horde of media until it was too late. Flashbulbs exploded around her like a New Year's light show. She skidded to a halt, so abruptly her trailing suitcase all but overtook her.

This had to be a case of mistaken identity. Surely. Kimberley hadn't been on the paparazzi hit list for close to a decade, not since she'd estranged herself from her billionaire father and his headline-hungry diamond business.

But no, it was *her* name they called. *Her* face was the focus of a swarm of lenses that circled her like avid hornets. Her heart started to pound with fear-fueled adrenaline.

What did they want?

What was going on?

With a rising sense of bewilderment she scanned the crowd for a clue, and her gaze fastened on a tall, leonine figure forcing his way to the front. A tall, familiar figure.

Her head came up in stunned recognition, and their gazes collided across the sea of heads before the cameras erupted with another barrage of flashes, this time right in her exposed face.

Blinded by the flashbulbs—and by the shock of that momentary eye-meet—Kimberley didn't realize his intent until he'd forged his way to her side, possibly by the sheer strength of his personality. She felt his arm wrap around her shoulder, pulling her into the protective shelter of his body, allowing her no time to object. No chance to lift her hands to ward him off.

In the space of a hastily drawn breath, she found herself plastered knee-to-nose against six feet two inches of hard-bodied male.

Ric Perrini.

Her lover for ten torrid weeks, her husband for ten tumultuous days.

Her ex for ten tranquil years.

After all this time, he should not have felt so familiar but, oh dear, he did. She knew the scent of that body and its lean, muscular strength. She knew its heat and its slick power and every response it could draw from hers.

She also recognized the ease with which he'd taken control of the moment and the decisiveness of his deep voice when it rumbled close to her ear. "I have a car waiting outside. Is this your only luggage?"

Kimberley nodded. "I assume you will tell me," she said tightly, "what this welcome party is all about."

"Not while the welcome party is within earshot. No."

Barking a request for the cameramen to stand aside, Perrini took her hand and pulled her into step with his ground-eating stride. Kimberley let him, because he was right, damn his arrogant, Italian-suited hide. Despite the speed with which he whisked her across the airport terminal, she could almost feel the hot breath of the pursuing media on her back.

This was neither the time nor the place for explanations. Inside his car, however, she would get answers.

Now that the initial shock had been blown away—by the haste of their retreat, by the heat of her gathering indignation, by the rush of adrenaline fired by Perrini's presence and the looming verbal battle—her brain was starting to tick over. This had to be her father's doing. And if it was a Howard Blackstone publicity ploy, then it had to be about Blackstone Diamonds, the company that ruled his life.

The knowledge made her chest tighten with a familiar ache of disillusionment.

She'd known her father would be flying in from Sydney for today's opening of the newest in his chain of exclusive, high-end jewelry boutiques. The opulent shopfront sat adjacent to the rival business where Kimberley worked. No coincidence, she thought bitterly, just as it was no coincidence that Ric Perrini was here in Auckland ushering her to his car.

Perrini was Howard Blackstone's right-hand man, second in command at Blackstone Diamonds, a legacy of his short-lived marriage to the boss's daughter. No doubt her father had sent him to fetch her; the question was *why?*

* * * * *

Get swept away down under with the glitz and glamour of the Blackstone empire as Kimberley tries to determine the real reason behind her "reunion" with Ric....

Look for VOWS & A VENGEFUL GROOM by Bronwyn Jameson, in stores January 2008.

Silhouette
Desire

When Kimberley Blackstone's father is
presumed dead, Kimberley is required to take
over the helm of Blackstone Diamonds. She
has to work closely with her ex, Ric Perrini, to
battle not only the press, but also the fierce
attraction still sizzling between them. Does Ric
feel the same...or is it the power her share of
Blackstone Diamonds will provide him as he
battles for boardroom supremacy.

Look for

VOWS &
A VENGEFUL GROOM

by

BRONWYN
JAMESON

Available January wherever you buy books

Visit Silhouette Books at www.eHarlequin.com   SD76843

Silhouette®

Desire

To fulfill his father's dying wish,
Greek tycoon Christos Niarchos must
marry Ava Monroe, a woman who
betrayed him years ago. But his soon-to-
be-wife has a secret that could rock
more than his passion for her.

Look for

THE GREEK TYCOON'S SECRET HEIR

by

KATHERINE GARBERA

Available January wherever you buy books

Visit Silhouette Books at www.eHarlequin.com   SD76845

Silhouette®

SPECIAL EDITION™

INTRODUCING A NEW 6-BOOK MINISERIES!

THE WILDER FAMILY
Healing Hearts in Walnut River

Walnut River's most prominent family,
the Wilders, are reunited in their struggle to
stop their small hospital from being taken over
by a medical conglomerate. Not only do they
find their family bonds again, they also find love.

STARTING WITH

FALLING FOR THE M.D.
by *USA TODAY*
bestselling author
MARIE FERRARELLA
January 2008

*Look for a book from The Wilder Family
every month until June!*

Visit Silhouette Books at www.eHarlequin.com   SSE24873

REQUEST YOUR FREE BOOKS!

2 FREE NOVELS PLUS 2
FREE GIFTS!

American **ROMANCE**®

Heart, Home & Happiness!

YES! Please send me 2 FREE Harlequin American Romance® novels and my 2 FREE gifts. After receiving them, if I don't wish to receive any more books, I can return the shipping statement marked "cancel." If I don't cancel, I will receive 4 brand-new novels every month and be billed just $4.24 per book in the U.S., or $4.99 per book in Canada, plus 25¢ shipping and handling per book and applicable taxes, if any*. That's a savings of close to 15% off the cover price! I understand that accepting the 2 free books and gifts places me under no obligation to buy anything. I can always return a shipment and cancel at any time. Even if I never buy another book from Harlequin, the two free books and gifts are mine to keep forever.

154 HDN EEZK   354 HDN EEZV

Name
(PLEASE PRINT)

Address
Apt. #

City
State/Prov.
Zip/Postal Code

Signature (if under 18, a parent or guardian must sign)

Mail to the **Harlequin Reader Service**®:
IN U.S.A.: P.O. Box 1867, Buffalo, NY 14240-1867
IN CANADA: P.O. Box 609, Fort Erie, Ontario L2A 5X3

Not valid to current Harlequin American Romance subscribers.

Want to try two free books from another line?
Call 1-800-873-8635 or visit www.morefreebooks.com.

* Terms and prices subject to change without notice. NY residents add applicable sales tax. Canadian residents will be charged applicable provincial taxes and GST. This offer is limited to one order per household. All orders subject to approval. Credit or debit balances in a customer's account(s) may be offset by any other outstanding balance owed by or to the customer. Please allow 4 to 6 weeks for delivery.

Your Privacy: Harlequin is committed to protecting your privacy. Our Privacy Policy is available online at www.eHarlequin.com or upon request from the Reader Service. From time to time we make our lists of customers available to reputable firms who may have a product or service of interest to you. If you would prefer we not share your name and address, please check here. ☐

HAR07

Inside ROMANCE

Stay up-to-date on all your
romance reading news!

Inside Romance is a FREE quarterly newsletter
highlighting our upcoming series releases
and promotions.

Visit
www.eHarlequin.com/InsideRomance
to sign up to receive our complimentary newsletter today!

IRNI107

HARLEQUIN *Presents*

Men who can't be tamed...or so they think!

If you love strong, commanding men—
you'll love this brand-new miniseries.

Meet the guy who breaks the rules to get exactly
what he wants, because he is...

HARD-EDGED & HANDSOME
He's impossible to resist....

RICH & RAKISH
He's got everything and needs nobody....
Until he meets one woman...

RUTHLESS
In his pursuit of passion; in his world the winner takes all!

THE ITALIAN BILLIONAIRE'S
RUTHLESS REVENGE
by Jacqueline Baird
Book #2693

Guido Barberi hasn't set eyes on his ex-wife since she left him.
He will have revenge by making her his mistress....
Can she resist his campaign of seduction?

If you love a darkly gorgeous hero,
look out for more Ruthless books, coming soon!

Brought to you by your favorite Harlequin Presents authors!

www.eHarlequin.com   HP12693

HARLEQUIN®

INTRIGUE®

INTRIGUE'S ULTIMATE HEROES

★

6 heroes. 6 stories.
One month to read them all.

For one special month, Harlequin Intrigue
is dedicated to those heroes among men.
Desirable doctors, sexy soldiers, brave
bodyguards—they are all
Intrigue's Ultimate Heroes.

In January, collect all 6.

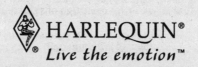

HARLEQUIN®
Live the emotion™

www.eHarlequin.com   HI69302

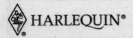

HARLEQUIN®

American ★ Romance®

COMING NEXT MONTH

#1193 A RANDALL HERO by Judy Christenberry
When John Randall swerved to avoid a broken-down car on a deserted Rawhide,
Wyoming, road, the cowboy never dreamed he'd find a beautiful woman inside.
Like a knight without his steed, John came to her rescue. He had no choice.
Lucy Horton was on the run...and about to give birth.

#1194 FAMILY BY DESIGN by Roxann Delaney
Motherhood
Becca Tyler stomped on Nick Morelli's heart once—for all the wrong reasons.
Now the boy from the wrong side of the tracks is a successful builder, while the
high school golden girl is a single mom just scraping by. Although the spark of
their first love still glows, a secret Nick is keeping could ruin the lovers' reunion
before it begins....

#1195 GOOD HUSBAND MATERIAL by Kara Lennox
Fatherhood
The last thing Natalie Briggs needed in her hectic life was to run into her sexy
ex-husband at their twenty-fifth high school reunion! But when a romantic
night of lovemaking leads to an unexpected pregnancy, life gets even *more*
complicated. They split over child-related issues before...is this their second
chance to start a family?

#1196 EMMY AND THE BOSS by Penny McCusker
Nick Porter really hadn't wanted to hire an efficiency expert, but to secure a
bank loan to save his company, he had to put up with Emmy Jones. He was
expecting a suit-wearing, briefcase-toting uptight drill-sergeant type...Emmy
was anything but. Who knew an efficiency expert would come in such a pretty
package?

www.eHarlequin.com

HARCNM1207